The Ba

AMETHYST HUE

Cover by
Hammad Khalid
(hmd_gfx)

...For Rachel and Abe Lincoln

CONTENTS

ACKNOWLEDGMENTS

The author acknowledges the support of family and friends throughout the writing of this book.

PROLOGUE

Sweaty and out of breath, Luther darted amongst the shadows trying to reach his apartment off Woodlawn. His handsome features were concealed by his oversized hoodie, but worry marred his nut-brown eyes. Standing furtively in an alley, he paused to catch his breath. Sitting the heavy duffel bag on the ground beside him, he scanned the area for any sign of a police car. He was almost home and he could see his apartment from his huddled position. He'd chosen the four-story building because it was quiet, near campus and near the El. But at one o'clock in the morning on a weekend, his normally quiet street was teeming with carousing students. Assuming a jovial nonchalant stance, he emerged from the shadows and ambled the short distance to his building. The duffel bag he carried tightly in his hand was a grim reminder of what he'd volunteered to do and how badly he had botched things.

All that blood, he shuddered, as he staggered into the lobby. Breathing another sigh of relief to find the lobby empty, he bounded up the stairs. So far so good, he thought, slipping the key in the lock. Entering his studio apartment, he was shocked to find his normally ordered space in complete disarray. Everything had been tossed haphazardly about. The locked file where he kept his notes had been forced open and its contents removed.

Pacing the disordered chaos, he tried to think rationally. He was in over his head, he conceded. He needed help; and a place to hold up until things quieted down.

"Raven!" he gasped fumbling wildly for the phone. Punching in the number, he dropped the receiver when the high-pitched whine of a police siren pierced the night air. For a moment, he stood there not knowing what to do. As the siren faded into the distance, he was galvanized into action. Snatching up the duffel bag, he dashed out the door.

ONE

Raven woke to loud agitated knocking on her door. She lived in a brownstone just north of the Field Museum; and had always felt safe in the South Loop. But waking to some maniac banging on your door at the crack of dawn, would scare the bejeezus out of anyone, she fumed. The clock on the night stand read 6 a.m. At this time of day, it couldn't be anyone she knew, she thought crossly. Burrowing deeper under her warm comforter, she tried to ignore the idiot, who was undoubtedly at the wrong door. But the nut job continued to pound on her door demanding admittance. Too tense to sleep, Raven flinched with each loud thump inflicted on her door. When the psycho began to rattle the door handle, she'd had enough. Feeling like slapping whoever was out there, she crawled out of bed and padded wearily to the door.

"Who is it?" she yawned.

"The police open up!" was bellowed aggressively from the other side. Looking through the peephole, Raven saw a badge shoved menacingly towards the opening. All she could make out was gold lettering which read Chicago Police Dept.

"Great," she groaned quietly. Stepping back, she opened the door a miniscule crack.

Detective Maverick Reid saw a wary brown eye peer out at him questioningly. "Raven Jahoda?" he barked.

Who wants to know, she demanded silently? Taking an instant and intense dislike to the man, she replied cautiously with, "yes."

"I'd like to ask you some questions."

"What about?"

"Your brother, Luther Jahoda."

Closing the door, Raven took off the security chain. The detective sauntered lazily into her apartment.

"What's this about?" she asked woodenly.

Inviting him no further than the doorstep, she was too stressed to give him more than a cursory glance. She saw only a tall white man with broad shoulders. She failed to take in his rugged good looks, athletic physique or deep umber eyes; eyes that could darken with the intensity of his passion or lighten with his ever-present mirth. She was immediately defensive having a cop in her home and folding her arms across her chest, she glared at him belligerently.

The pint-sized woman trying to stare him down did not intimidate Detective Reid. His wide sensual lips pressed in a grim line began to soften as he looked down at her. She was more than a foot shorter than his 6'4 frame, he surmised. Dressed in warm lavender long johns, she looked adorable he mused. Her creamy brown skin had the subtle scent of vanilla. When her tongue snaked out to nervously moisten her lips, his eyes zeroed in on the gesture. She was trying to glare at him with bluff and bravado. But he'd seen her eyes widen with fear at the mention of her brother. Raven Jahoda knew something, and he planned to get it out of her.

"I'm Detective Maverick Reid," he introduced with a friendly smile. But Raven standing there like a stone Buddha, continued to stare at him aggressively. "My friends call me Mac," he offered extending his hand.

Gazing at the proffered hand as if he was asking her to touch something slimy and wiggly, Raven tried to get her heartbeat under control. Stalling for time, she ran her hand nervously through her hair. Unfortunately, this knocked the scrunchie holding it in a precarious knot to the floor. Thick black curls cascaded around her shoulders. Raven felt like a space cadet as she bent to retrieve the scrunchie. Mac watching her every move, silently noted that she looked tired. She was also far too sexy to be standing before him in long johns, he decided. The thermal attire encased her body like a second skin. His eyes widened in appreciation at the swell of full breasts and flat abdomen enticingly displayed.

"If you'd like to get a bathrobe I can wait," he suggested, looking pointedly at her breasts.

Thoroughly embarrassed, Raven turned swiftly and headed for her bedroom. Berating herself unmercifully for parading around like a shameless hussy; she missed Mac's barely audible gasp of appreciation, at her firm tight derrière retreating down the hall. Dressing quickly Raven returned to the living room. She expected to find the detective waiting patiently by the front door. But he was bending over her desk on the other side of the room. He was trying to decipher a note she'd scribbled on the phone pad.

"What are you doing?" she demanded worriedly.

"Investigating," Mac replied turning slowly. Giving her the once over, he saw she'd changed into jeans and a cream cropped sweater. The sweater fit snugly around her breasts, and left a tiny portion of her mid-section exposed. He allowed his eyes to cut a leisurely swath across her body. This outfit was sexier than her long john attire, he thought; plus, her exposed mid-section was damn distracting. Mac knew Raven was 27 years old, because he'd had her under surveillance for months; but without make up, she looked younger and very vulnerable. She was also starting to get uncomfortable with his silent appraisal so he lowered his eyes to her bare feet.

Ignoring the tension his intense appraisal generated, Raven cleared her throat and walked slowly towards the desk. Discretely ripping the message from the phone pad, she slipped it in her pocket and asked, "was Luther in an accident or s...something?"

Smooth, Mac thought at her attempt to feign innocence. If it hadn't been for her slight stutter on the word something, he might be inclined to believe she didn't know about Juanita. "We have reason to believe Luther was heavily involved with a Juanita Ellison," Mac announced; watching her reactions closely.

Folding her arms across her chest again, Raven murmured, "so."

"Did you know her?"

"Vaguely," she lied moving towards the window.

"We believe they were together last night."

"Um," she nodded; hoping she was projecting an air of benign interest. She hadn't known Luther was seeing anyone, let alone this Juanita Ellison person.

"She was murdered," Mac announced bluntly. Observing the stunned shock Raven was unable to suppress, he waited for her vehement denial of Luther's involvement. But other than squaring her shoulders, as if bracing herself for more bad news, Raven didn't answer. "It's possible Luther may know something about the case," Mac persisted. When she continued to stare at him mutely, he said, "we have some questions we'd like to ask him."

"I'm sure he's at home this time of day…" she began.

"He's not," Mac interrupted with a shake of his head.

"Did you check the campus science lab?"

"We did, he's not there."

"Well he's not here either."

"Do you know where he is?"

"He could be with his lab partner."

"Gary Randall?" Mac asked checking his notes. When she nodded, he said, "we have not been able to locate him either."

"So," she uttered.

"Do you have any means of locating Gary?"

"Other than calling his apartment?" she queried sarcastically. At his oblique nod, she informed him curtly, "no."

Quirking an eyebrow in her direction, he asked, "and his apartment is where?"

"He lives in the grad apartments; just off campus."

"When's the last time you saw him?"

"A while ago," Raven answered with an airy wave of her hand. Trying to look bored with the situation, she said, "he tagged along with Luther to some family function about four months ago."

"And you don't know where Luther is now?"

"No," she shrugged.

Cocking his head to observe her dubiously, Mac digested this skeptically. "You know withholding information in a police investigation is a felony," he replied almost conversationally.

"Luther isn't here," Raven sputtered. "I don't know where he is."

She was visibly shaken, Mac saw as she turned towards the window. With a hand that shook slightly, she reached for the cord to open the drapes. The sun rising over the horizon was beautiful. But the woman trying to buy some time, by finagling an excuse to open the drapes, did not fool him. He knew she was trying to compose herself, by pretending to take great interest in the scenic view.

"Phone records show Luther called your number a little after one o'clock this morning," he continued. Closing her eyes briefly, Raven tried to contain the shudder rippling through her body. "It shouldn't be too hard to get a warrant to search the premises."

"Then get one!" she challenged turning to glare at him aggressively.

"Look Raven," he began. Feeling the waves of hostility rolling off her small frame, he decided to change tactics. Assuming a nonchalant stance, he asked, "may I call you Raven?"

"No!" she declared hotly. "That's Nubian

12

Princess to you!" At the absurdity of this request, Mac couldn't help himself. His lips began to twitch before he gave himself up to genuine laughter.

"Alright...er...Nubian," he stressed. "May I be so bold as to request a mere cup of coffee for these humble lips? I've been working this case all night and I'm beat."

"You're the one that barged in here..." she began. Her voice fizzled out when she noticed how exhausted he looked. His eyes were red rimmed and his face was heavily lined with stress. "Fine," she reluctantly agreed as he shifted out of his coat. "But I don't have any donuts."

The snide dig at his profession did not go unnoticed by Mac and he smiled briefly before saying, "just coffee is fine." Sitting on a barstool, he watched as she maneuvered around her galley styled kitchen preparing coffee.

"I only have instant," she grudgingly admitted.

"Instant's fine," he murmured. Running his hand tiredly through his thick brown hair, he frowned slightly at the dull ache in his head. He needed to find Luther, he mused. Find him before the press mangled the story and whipped the city into a fanatical frenzy of police brutality against the black man. The situation called for delicacy, not blunt media force. Shrewdly monitoring Raven's jerky movements, Mac knew she could be the key to where Luther was hiding. But teasing the information out of her wasn't going to be easy. It was quite obvious that having a detective in her midst was entirely new territory for her. She was scared and with the right pressure, she'd crack he observed with a wry twist of his lips. Sometimes he really didn't like his job; he realized, as she placed a steaming cup of coffee in front of him. Frowning when she scuttled to the far end of the kitchen to eye him warily, he decided to proceed.

"How long have you lived in this apartment?" he asked solicitously.

Thrown by the question, Raven stared at him suspiciously. What was he up to now, she wondered? "I've been here three years," she answered cautiously.

"The South Loop is a good location," he offered. "Mature trees, back to nature, the view from here is great."

"Uh...Yeah," she nodded. Still unsure where he was going with this new line of questioning, she stared at him discerningly. But he was giving nothing away; if anything, his features became more guarded as he directed his gaze out the window. Following his gaze, Raven silently marveled at the scene. From her apartment, she had a panoramic view of Grant Park. In the autumn like now it was a wonder to behold. But why was a policeman discussing it with her like they were old friends? She'd have to be stupid to forget why he was really in her apartment. He was trying to incriminate Luther. Either that or plant evidence, she feared.

Feeling trapped, she blurted, "Luther is getting his PH.D. He attends the University of Chicago. He doesn't break the law."

"We just want to ask him some questions and dismiss him as a suspect."

"He's a suspect?" she questioned clearly alarmed.

"Routine procedure," Mac soothed. "At this stage in the investigation everyone's a suspect. Juanita was killed around midnight. Where were you around midnight?"

"In bed sleeping."

"Alone?" Mac queried.

"No. I was with a legion of angry black men!" she snapped sarcastically.

"You do know that a legion is a thousand?" he asked with a raised eyebrow.

"Two legions then," Raven corrected with a slight shrug.

"In other words, you don't have an alibi for your whereabouts around midnight?" Nodding curtly, she glared at him stonily. "Witnesses report a man fitting Luther's description fleeing the scene." When she continued to stare at him mutinously, he heaved, "we can do this here or downtown Raven."

"Downtown?" she practically shouted with rising hysteria. "Am I being charged with a crime? I don't know where Luther is! I haven't seen him in…um…in…months!"

"This isn't going to go away," he stressed. "A girl was killed. We need to find Luther."

"If I see him, I'll tell him you're looking for him," she mouthed flippantly.

"The law guarantees everyone due process," he replied.

"Yeah, right!" Raven snorted sarcastically. Mac was well aware of the immense distrust the black community had in regards to police officers. Arguing with her wasn't going to change that. The muted ringing of her cell phone had her lunging across the room with a guilty start. Her look of real fear as she cupped the receiver to her ear had Mac surmising Luther had to be the caller.

"I can't talk now," she blabbed nervously into the receiver. "I'm with the police now."

Breaking the connection, she quickly stuffed the phone in her pants pocket.

"Was that Luther?" Mac asked.

"No!" she declared too aggressively. Recognizing her mistake, she quickly amended, "I mean…uh…no…that was a friend."

"Whether you believe me or not Raven, I'm trying to help Luther. The sooner he makes contact with me the better." Draining his coffee cup, he rose from the barstool. Taking out his card, he placed it on the counter with, "all police officers are not gunning for young black males." Gazing at her upturned face, he could tell she didn't believe him. "I'll be in touch," he said before taking his leave.

TWO

The stench reeking from the dank dilapidated building in Lawndale, had Raven gagging in disgust. The building had to be mold infested and possibly rat infested as well, she blenched. She'd followed Luther's instructions explicitly. After waiting several hours, she'd headed out. To insure no one was following her; she'd taken several benign bus rides around Chicago. Four cross town buses later, she'd finally taken the El to North Lawndale.

"Ugh," she shuddered staring at the tumble-down shack of an apartment building. Luther had to be in deep doo to end up in a place like this, she grimaced. Urban renewal was slowly tearing down or revamping broken down buildings. But there was a good way to go, before the project was complete. Chicago still had thousands of derelict or abandoned buildings around town; in varying stages of wood rot. The one she was in seemed to be the worst of the bunch, Raven thought. Searching for the name, Lenny Poe on the mailbox; she half expected not to find it. She wasn't sure if she was relieved or scared to see, L. Poe 3-D scrawled in small letters on the second row of graffiti marred boxes.

It was a wonder city ordinance permitted anyone to occupy this dump, she cringed, as she crept slowly up the stairs. Broken beer bottles and urine seemed to be everywhere and she tried not to touch or step in anything. Reaching the third floor landing, Raven nervously approached apartment D and rapped sharply on the door.

"Who is it?" was growled softly from the other side. She breathed a sigh of relief when recognizing Luther's voice.

"It's me," she murmured. Leaning towards the door, she looked furtively around to insure no one heard her. As locks were thrown, she listened tensely for any sound that would alert her to danger. Concentrating on the sounds around her, she was unprepared when an arm suddenly snaked out and yanked her unceremoniously into the apartment. Stumbling awkwardly across the threshold, she took a moment to get her bearing. Aside from a small table and two rickety chairs; the only furniture in the dimly lit room was a bed that had hit its prime sometime during the Dark Ages.

Regaining her footing as the door was slammed and locked behind her she said, "I don't know what kind of a mess you've gotten yourself into Luther, but the poli…" Turning to find Mac leaning casually against the locked door, her mouth hung open in complete shock. Dressed as he was in homeless attire, she'd recognize him anywhere. His slumberous stance belied the angry glare in his intense umber gaze. Stunned Raven tried to voice her horror at finding him in the apartment. Her mouth worked frantically, but no words came out. What was he doing here, she wondered?

"You have any idea the kind of danger you put yourself in by coming here?" he growled in a menacing whisper.

"I… how…" was all Raven managed to articulate as she stared at him with deeply shocked eyes.

"I learned to read scribble in high school," he answered her unspoken question. "I can also read upside down and backwards," he added when she continued to stare at him stunned and bemused.

"But just now…through the door you

sounded like…"

"Like who?" he challenged.

"Um…no one," she murmured awkwardly.

"I can also do a fairly good rendition of Santa," Mac enlightened, mimicking Luther's voice to the letter.

"You know Luther?" Raven accused as comprehension dawned.

"Naturally," he drawled in Luther's voice again.

Hearing Luther's voice coming out of Mac's mouth was very disconcerting. Wincing, she uttered, "stop doing that. It's creeping me out."

"So, you don't know Luther's whereabouts hmmm?" he questioned with a raised eyebrow.

"I don't," Raven answered deciding to bluff her way out of the situation. Shrugging her shoulders, she observed him with disdain. "I was meeting a friend here for a late lunch," she offered. "And I can sue you for man handling a private citizen," she informed him. Belatedly massaging her arm to emphasize his rough treatment when he'd yanked her inside the apartment, she said, "this isn't the 1960s and you can't push people around. Don't make me get a lawyer," she threw in for good measure.

Smiling in spite of himself, Mac had to admire her spunk. Here she was alone in a seedy section of town, in an almost abandoned building, threatening him with a lawsuit. The girl had guts, he'd give her that much. "Apartment 3-D has special meaning for you then?" he asked.

"It's my old stomping ground," she scoffed.

"Really," he derided skeptically. "Because I'm pretty sure Luther grew up in Gurnee."

"Where?" Raven murmured.

"Gurnee, Illinois." Mac repeated. "You know that highfalutin suburb of Chicago. It's about 45 miles from here."

"Never heard of it," she dismissed with a slight shrug.

"I just figured you might know exactly where it is; seeing as how you and Luther grew up together," Mac emphasized. "Plus, you don't have the verbiage or dialect from this neighborhood," he commented looking her up and down. "You practically speak the King's English. Your speech is way too proper and…"

"I don't think a white American male is in any position to talk to me about Ebonics, or linguistics of any kind that pertains to the African American culture," Raven interjected.

"See, phrases like pertains to," Mac pointed out, as if he was teaching a class in *English As A Second Language*. "No one in this neighborhood says pertains to. Also, you don't have that notable shoulder chip that is so often associated with this hood."

"Whatever," Raven responded dully. Did he know she was there because she'd received a frantic call from Luther asking for help? Trying to discern from his expression how much he knew; she wondered if he had seen Luther in the vicinity of the building. Maybe Luther had approached the building, spotted Mac and left.

"This is a hangout for drug users," Mac snarled harshly watching her flinch.

"Luther is not a drug user!" Raven voiced emphatically. She didn't realize she'd walked right into his trap until his eyes lit in triumph at her admission. "I mean," she corrected lamely; "whoever was staying here is most likely an innocent bystander."

"Most like," he agreed in a feeble attempt at Ebonics.

"So, um… did you see who was here or anything?"

The question was asked with a false sense of casualness, Mac observed. But he could see fear gathering in the depths of her brown eyes, that Luther may have been exposed and hauled off to the slammer.

"Luther has not been arrested if that's what you're getting at," he remarked. "As far as I know, he's still at large."

"Who?" Raven asked with beguiling innocence.

"Your brother," Mac chuckled at her feigned innocent act.

"Oh, him…right…right," she nodded as if she'd just recalled she had a sibling. "I'm just here waiting for my friend; uh, Tall-girl."

"Really?" Mac snickered thoroughly amused. "You're actually going to go with a name as weak as Tall-girl? As fake names go, that one is seriously lame," he chortled.

"Tall-girl happens to be her name."

"And why, may I ask, is she called Tall-girl?"

"Because she was 5'7" in the fifth grade."

"How tall is she now; seven feet?" he guessed.

"She's my height, about 5'10."

"You're not 5'10," Mac corrected. "You're

about 5'3."

"Yeah, but in heels Tall-girl and I…."

"You can't count the height acquired from a six inch heel as your own," he announced smugly.

"Who died and made you king of the tall people?" Raven rejoined.

"Good lord," he chortled with genuine amusement, "you have height issues."

"Shut up," Raven grimaced; in part because there may have been a tiny granule of truth in his statement.

"My bad," he offered making no effort to hide his amusement.

"I guess you should be going then?"

"That's alright. I'll wait here with you."

"No!" Raven insisted not wanting him anywhere near the building should Luther arrive. "Feel free to take off. I'm sure you have policeman stuff to do, people to arrest, donuts to eat."

"Nah," he responded moving to sit in one of the rickety chairs. It groaned heavily under his weight but it held him; much to Raven's chagrin. "I'll sit with you and wait for this Tall-girl person," he replied. Rolling his eyes sarcastically, he admitted, "I'm dying to meet someone with such an eclectic name."

"Look detective Reid that won't be…"

"Mac," he interrupted.

"Huh?"

"Call me Mac," he invited.

Nodding curtly Raven informed him haughtily, "I can take care of myself. I'm over 21 and no longer a slave. I'm free to wait…"

"You're going to play the race card throughout our relationship, aren't you?" he smiled.

"We don't have a relationship."

Seated, Mac was on eye level with her and she was able to see what could have been admiration or possibly desire burning in his eyes. Either way, he was making no effort to hide it she noted. "Once this mess with Luther is cleared up, we will definitely have a relationship," he promised.

"I thought you were convinced Luther was guilty."

"I never said that," he reminded her. "You got your back up the moment I crossed your threshold."

"Well if you had started the conservation with Luther's innocent."

"And would you have believed me?" he asked eyeing her askance.

"Well no," she admitted. "But it wouldn't have hurt."

"Let's go," he said reaching for her hand.

"Where?" she asked pulling back.

"My place I want to shower and change."

"But what if Luther…"

"He's not coming," Mac supplied.

"Really?" Raven asked with an exaggerated lilt to her voice. Watching him suspiciously, she asked, "how do you know that?"

"Come with me and find out," he offered holding out his hand.

{}

Before leaving the apartment, Mac insisted on disguising her appearance. He explained that someone dressed as he was would draw too much attention from the locals; if seen with someone dressed as she was. He then proceeded to rough up her hair; before throwing a battered and completely trifling coat on her. The coat was in such a state that Raven felt it would have to work its way up to being a tattered rag. Turning her towards the mirror, Mac smiled when Raven cringed at her appearance. She looked like scrag-zilla. She asked Mac if she should walk hunched over with a limp. But he disagreed; stating that would draw too much attention. The key word, he instructed as they left the building, was incognito.

Raven tried not to visibly wince at the rattle trap of a car Mac lead her to. It was completely disfigured with rust; and looked like it had sat in an impound lot for decades. She freely admitted that a patrol car would have been far too conspicuous in this neighborhood; but even so, she had been expecting transportation that wasn't the equivalent of a prehistoric death trap. As Mac tried to coax the car into drive mode; it coughed and sputtered loudly, before it finally decided to end the drama and take its rightful place in traffic. Raven was sure that if an unattended tire rolled past their window, it would be from Mac's car. The pile of rust was shaking so badly as he gunned it up to the minimum driving speed on the highway; that she had to hold on to the seat tightly, just to keep from being knocked into the door.

"Smooth ride," she yelled sarcastically into the loud din as the car lumbered along. Mac didn't respond to her sarcasm because he clearly didn't hear her. Apparently, the man had no concept of the purpose of a muffler. If she incurred a noise induced hearing loss while riding in his rattle trap of a car, she was going to sue him; and take his stupid car and have it turned into a can opener. Gleefully caught up in Mac's humiliating demise through the court system; she was caught off guard when he pulled into the private enclave of a two story stone cedar style home in Lincoln Park. Surrounded by mature trees it was completely private. The back of the house was open to Lincoln Park. Its geometric design of floor to ceiling windows ensured year long enjoyment of the park's beauty. Raven was impressed by the sheer beauty of the place and asked in a surprised whisper, "where are we?"

"Lincoln Park," Mac replied pulling into the three car garage.

His rattle trap car was completely out of place in the opulent surroundings, Raven thought. Exiting the car, she removed the scrag-like coat and returned it to Mac. As he took the coat, she barely stopped herself from saying, good riddance with a dramatic shudder. Instead she admitted, "I know where we are. I meant who lives here?"

"I do."

"You live here?" she asked with blatant disbelief.

"Yep," he grinned at her look of skepticism.

An upscale quiet residential neighborhood did not fit the image she had of Mac. "You just don't strike me as a quiet residential street kind of guy," she voiced.

"Don't tell me," he derided with a raised eyebrow. "You see me living in a tree eating raw meat."

"Sometimes," Raven chuckled. "But mostly I had you pegged as a live in the now, near the action kind of guy. Somewhere like Wrigleyville or Wicker town…"

"In a tree?"

"A loft. Decorated in a trendy contemporary style."

"You like contemporary?"

"Hate it."

Smiling as if he approved of her answer, Mac replied, "Chicago is a big place. I need to get away from the action from time to time. I come here to unwind," he added with a stifled yawn. "Make yourself at home," he invited; guiding her to the hearth room. Her eyes were immediately drawn to the majestic fireplace which was shared by the dining room. Following her gaze, he drawled, "that's one of two double fireplaces in the house. Play your cards right and I'll show you the other one," he husked with a conspirator's wink.

But Raven was only half listening to his spiel. She was wondering how Mac could afford such a swank neighborhood on a policeman salary. Lincoln Park was one of the most desirable neighborhoods in Chicago. Its picturesque lakefront space and wide tree lined streets made it beautiful but also pricey.

"How can you afford this?" she asked baldly. "You work for the police department and they're always complaining about needing more money." The atmosphere of camaraderie evaporated immediately and Mac's face shuttered into hard granite. "I'm sorry. It's none of my business," she blabbed sensing she had somehow offended him.

"You're honest," he snapped harshly. "You say what you mean."

Starting to feel ill at ease when he continued to glare at her, Raven realized she actually knew next to nothing about Mac. For all she knew, he could be the culprit behind Juanita's death and Luther's disappearance. In fact, she reasoned, a pretty good case could be lobbied against him. He was at Luther's hideout. He could be trying to set Luther up by using her as a decoy.

"Have you finished convicting me?" Mac

asked through clinched teeth.

"I wasn't trying...I mean... I didn't mean...uh...I don't know what you're talking..."

Holding up a hand to stop her stilted assertions of innocence, he spat, "leave it!" Ripping the tattered toboggan from his head with an angry jerk of his hand he snarled, "wait here. I'll be back shortly."

THREE

Raven watched him go with an acute feeling of guilt. She'd hurt him. She hadn't meant to, but she obviously had. Sinking onto the sofa, she contemplated going after him. But what could she say, she wondered, with a wry twist of her lips. *Sorry I took you for a cold blooded killer*. He wouldn't believe her, if the expression on his face was anything to go by. Maybe she should change her name to open-mouth-insert-foot Jahoda. They could call her *Omif* for short, she thought with a rueful grin.

Absently restacking the magazines strewn across his coffee table, Raven decided Mac was a bit of a clutter bug. The room wasn't a disaster, but it definitely needed straightening up. Under the guise of re-organizing his clutter, she cautiously peeked in a drawer. She didn't know precisely what she was looking for. I mean it's not like she expected to find his detailed confession written out in long hand; or the murder weapon stained with his bloody prints. As she discretely searched his abode, she figured any clue was better than no clue. If he caught her in the act, she'd tell him she was de-cluttering his space. Ten minutes later, Raven conceded she was the worse snoop ever. Other than getting a bird's eye view of Mac's decorating scheme, she hadn't turned up anything useful about the case. His home was tastefully decorated in masculine hues of silver, black and gray; with the occasional splash of olive green. No doubt it was all done by a designer, she silently scoffed. Mac didn't strike her as a man who visited furniture stores or pored over swatches of fabric. What now, she grimaced when her cell phone began to vibrate? Raising it to her ear, she intoned wearily into the receiver, "yes?"

"Raven?" was husked hoarsely down the line.

"Luther!" she yelped almost dropping the phone. Fully alert now, she asked, "what happened? You weren't at the apartment."

"I was tracking down a new lead. Can you meet me at your place in half an hour?"

"I'm in Lincoln Park and I don't have my car with me. I can't make it to my place in…."

"Can you try?" He urged.

"I'm leaving now," she sighed. Sorely tempted to roll her eyes in a gesture of long-suffering, Raven raced towards the door. She let out a startled scream when Mac suddenly appeared in the doorway. His hair was slicked back from his shower and water beaded seductively across his broad shoulders. If she hadn't been so rattled, she probably would have noticed how unbearably sexy he was; wearing only a towel draped loosely around his rugged hips. As it was, she only noticed that with his arms folded firmly across his expansive chest, he effectively barred the way out.

"Mac!" she declared with her hand over her rapidly beating heart; "you scared me half to death springing out like that."

"Who were you talking to?" he asked. Homing in on the phone held tightly in her hand, he watched her closely.

"What?" she mumbled.

"You were talking to someone," he commented reaching out to examine the readout.

Glancing at the phone, Raven felt tremendous relief that Luther had broken the connection. She wouldn't put it past Mac to push the received call button, somehow use the URL to find Luther's location. Before he could do that, she snapped her phone shut and uttered, "I um... I need to leave. Something has come up."

"What's the big emergency?" he asked skeptically.

"It's personal." Raven mumbled, trying to ease past him. But Mac shifted his position, and once again blocked her escape route.

"Let me give you a lift," he offered cordially. But Raven wasn't fooled. She had no trouble deciphering the speculative gleam in his eyes. He suspected she was on her way to see Luther and was trying to horn in on the deal.

"That won't be necessary. I'm just going home...I...um...need to feed my cat."

Staring at her for several long seconds, Mac finally replied softly, "you don't have any cats." Watching her swallow fearfully, he immediately regretted commenting on such an intimate detail of her life. Now she knew he'd run a thorough check on her; even down to the pet, or lack thereof, that she owned. Good job Mac, he silently reproved. Way to ease the paranoia and gain the trust. Sighing in frustration, he murmured, "give me a chance to get dressed, and I'll take you home."

Instinctively stepping back when he took a step towards her, she replied, "uh…no…no…I'm fine. I'll...um…just catch the El."

"What hideous lies has Luther been feeding you Raven?"

"What?" she asked inching further away.

"You were fine a minute ago. One phone call and you're as jittery as a cat facing a pack of rabid pit bulls. What does Luther want you to do now?"

"This has nothing to do with Luther," Raven insisted. "I just find it odd to be standing next to a naked man when I'm fully clothed."

"That can easily be remedied," Mac grinned reaching for her.

"There will be no remedying of anything," Raven uttered batting his hands away. "And could you please put some clothes on."

"Why?" he drawled ruefully. "Does it bother you that I'm totally commando under this towel?"

"Not even a little," she lied.

"We'll see about that," he murmured as he closed the gap between them. He was so close now; Raven could feel the heat from his body.

"What are you doing?" she demanded in an alarmed yelp.

"An experiment," Mac husked as he gathered her into his arms. Standing so close, he could feel the tremors; she was desperately trying to hide, coursing through her body. She was scared of him. After the steps he'd taken not to alarm her with the details of Luther's involvement, she was back to being as tense as a bow string. "You can trust me Raven," he rumbled deep in his chest.

Could she, she wondered finding his tone surprisingly comforting. She'd been on edge since Luther phoned in the wee hours of the morning, alerting her to his situation. She could do with some comfort, she thought. Sighing with contentment, she closed her eyes and rested her head against his chest. When Mac felt some of the tension ease from her body, his eyes glittered in triumph.

Drawing her closer still he murmured softly, "what did Luther tell you?"

Stunned she was being comforted by a potential enemy, Raven drew herself up rigidly and jerked out of his embrace. She wasn't about to question the psychological ramifications of finding comfort in the arms of a probable killer. One hug and she was dangerously close to telling him whatever he wanted to know, she thought in disgust.

"I need to go," she said trying to slip past him.

Stopping her progression by gently capturing her arm, he said, "let me take you to dinner. We can clear up a few things over a nice relaxing dinner."

"I don't know," she hedged. "I'm meeting Lut…." Looking at Mac aghast, she stopped in mid-sentence. What was the matter with her, she wondered? Even if Mac wasn't somehow involved in all this, he was still a cop, she acknowledged silently. Yet here she was about to drop a dime on her own brother.

Watching her inner struggle, Mac felt his heart constrict with remorse. Luther really should have kept her out of all this. Dragging Raven into a game she didn't understand and was ill equipped to deal with was brutal. His gut tightened in anger whenever he thought of her showing up alone, at apartment 3D. Watching her closed expression, Mac admitted that if he hadn't deciphered her scribbled note, he would not have thought to go to the apartment. As it was, he'd only gotten there a mere half hour before she had. She was now a part of this; whether she wanted to be or not, he realized. The safest place for her was by his side.

"Wait here," he advised drawing her to the

sofa. Settling her carefully he murmured, "it'll only take me a minute to dress, and then I'll take you home."

Nodding acquiesce, Raven watched him go. She'd had a long and eventful day. All she really wanted was to go home to the cozy comfort of her own apartment. Opening her cell phone, she quickly sent Luther a text that Mac was bringing her home. She knew, he was sensible enough not to be there when they arrived.

{}

"You look like hell," Tall-girl announced abruptly upon entering Raven's apartment. She was struggling with several bags of Thai food and she went directly to the kitchen. Sitting the bags on the kitchen counter, she turned to Raven with an exaggerated scowl. "You owe me," she declared. "You know I hate going to Chinatown this time of day. Traffic is murder right now."

Raven had to smile at that one because Tall-girl loved nothing better than the hustle and bustle of city life. But she was never called Tall-girl these days. Born in Taiwan, she had taken the American name of Ashley. Raven had given Mac, Ashley's long dead school nickname, in an effort to keep him off her scent. Nowadays, most people just called her Ash. Ash was completely Americanized; and rarely used her given name of Ming-Win. Ash had sleek black hair and full lips. She was model thin; with an appetite like a rhinoceros and the metabolism of a humming bird.

"You didn't have to go to Chinatown Ash," Raven murmured taking plates and glasses from the cupboard. 'You could have gone to The Rice Bowl, that's right near you?"

"Your message said emergency. That means Spicy Thai Chicken. They don't carry Thai chicken at the Rice Bowl," she commented as she removed their delicious dinner from the bags.

"Not to mention your obsession with the seafood pot at Thai Palace," Raven snickered.

"Anyway," Ash continued as if Raven hadn't spoken, "what's the big emergency?"

"I'm having the weekend from hell," Raven heaved. "One more iota of stress… just one more… and I will start body slamming people."

As she spooned steamed rice on a plate, Ash replied sarcastically, "if we actually had a nickel for all of your body slamming threats, we'd be multi-millionaires by now."

Taking the plate laden with spicy Thai chicken from her, Raven asked, "don't you mean I would be a multi-millionaire… not we?"

"I'm your manager," she boasted.

"Since when?"

"Since now," she informed Raven in a no nonsense tone of voice. This got both of them laughing hysterically and Raven felt herself relax for the first time that day. She'd called Ash the second Mac had dropped her off. She needed a degree of normalcy back in her life and Ash most definitely brought that. Truth be told, Luther and Ash had been flirting with each other for years. But neither had made any serious inroads towards a relationship with each other. Raven had always thought Ash would make a great sister-in-law. As she ate a fork full of Thai chicken, she realized, Ash was already a big part of the Jahoda family. She'd make a better addition to the family than this Juanita person, Raven decreed with narrowed eyes. Of course, anyone would be better than a corpse….

"Yo Raven!" Ash bellowed waving her soup spoon dramatically in Raven's face. "I've asked you the same question twice, and you are completely ignoring me. What's going on with you?"

"Oh… sorry," Raven apologized. "What did you ask?"

"I asked why you were frowning. I thought

Thai chicken was your favorite."

"It is," Raven agreed. "It's just a little spicy."

"Really," Ash commented dubiously. "You were looking kinda intense for spicy food."

"Okay fine," Raven lied. "I'm worried about this upcoming exhibit."

"That again," Ash responded with pursed lips. "Since you got on at the museum, it's taken all the fun out of you. You practically live at that place."

"Not true," Raven responded. "Last weekend…"

"You bailed on our pedicure because of work last weekend," Ash reminded. "And today, you didn't show at the Arboretum for seeding. You're the one who got me started as a volunteer at the Arb, and you don't show."

"Ugh!" Raven moaned slapping her forehead. She'd forgotten about her volunteer stint. She and Ash did three hours shifts twice a month at Morton Arboretum and it had completely slipped her mind. What with Luther's phone call and Mac's visit, it was little wonder that was all she missed, she sighed.

"Where were you?" Ash asked.

"North Lawndale," Raven said casually.

"Lawndale! Get out! Who do you know in Lawndale?"

"I was looking for Luther."

"And why pray tell is Luther hanging out in Lawndale?"

She couldn't tell her Raven realized gazing at Ash closely. Before today, Raven was positive all signs pointed towards Ash and Luther becoming a couple. Raven didn't have the heart to tell her that apparently, Luther was sneaking around seeing Juanita Ellison. A Juanita Ellison who just happened to be a corpse; and Luther just happened to be a clear person of interest in her death. Nope, Raven decided; best to wait until she had more facts before she went down that road.

"I'm not sure," Raven answered truthfully.

FOUR

Surrounded by boxes of West African art, Raven massaged her temples tiredly. She'd covered the short distance from her apartment to the Museum in less than ten minutes. Not in the mood for the cheery gaiety of her co-workers, she'd successfully avoided most of the office staff. Now sitting on a workbench in the stock room, she only had Stella to deal with. When Charles strode unobtrusively into the room, she silently corrected; make that Stella and her faithful lap dog, Charles. Stella and Charles were always together and their friendship made no sense. While Stella was vivacious and vibrant; Charles was completely nondescript. His soft brown eyes, gently tanned skin and pudgy physique made it too easy to forget him. The man worked in receiving, but Raven used that term loosely. He was always in the stock room.

He followed Stella around like a puppy. If she said jump, he said how high.

"Hey guys, how's it going," he greeted. Taking a seat, he cozied up to Stella for a chummy chat.

Nodding in acknowledgement of his greeting, Raven tried to clear her head. She freely admitted, Mac had scared the stuffing out of her with his allegations about Luther. The entire affair was just too bizarre for words. Luther involved in a murder; get real, she silently scoffed. Luther wouldn't hurt a fly. He was studying forensic science for Pete's sake. He was planning to work in law enforcement. If the great detective had done his homework, he would have…

"Where were you this weekend?" Stella suddenly blared. Watching Raven intently, she said, "I called several times but you never answered the phone. Were you with Luther?"

Surprised Raven looked up to stare at her assistant shrewdly. She noticed absently that Charles was sitting dejectedly on the far side of the bench; a clear indication Stella had given him the brush off. Stella had been her assistant for nearly a year; and although they worked well together, they were not friends. The entire museum staff knew that telling Stella anything was the equivalent of putting up a flashing billboard on the highway.

Plus, her interest in what everyone did away from work boarded on ghoulish. Raven had often thought this ghoulish trait of hers was out of character with her overall persona. Stella wasn't bland or boring. There was no need for her to live vicariously through others, Raven reasoned.

Observing her assistant discretely, Raven concluded, Stella was sexy. Not only that, she had no qualms about displaying her body to its full advantage. As per usual, she was dressed as a typical sex kitten. Wearing tight fitting black jeans, a figure hugging burnt orange sweater and black stiletto-heeled ankle boots, she'd caught the eye of every heterosexual male in the museum. Even without her generous display of cleavage; her thick copper brown hair worn feathered to her shoulders, almond brown skin and full lips, put her in the attractive category. She was also open and aggressive about what she wanted, and went after it with gusto. But it was her unreasonable hatred and distrust of policemen; especially white policemen, that had Raven holding her tongue about Mac. The last thing she needed to hear right now was Stella's tally sheet of police brutality against the black man in Chicago.

"Were you with Luther?" Stella repeated with a furrowed brow.

"Oooooh Luther," Charles squealed perking

up. Taking the opportunity to scoot closer to Stella, he asked, "what's Luther up to now? He's always into something," he mouthed at Stella.

Yay me, Raven inwardly cringed, another gossip hound. With a mental eye roll, she decided the two of them were going to drive her to drink.

"Er…No… I wasn't with Luther. I had a lot of running around to do," Raven responded. Applying a crowbar to the crate in front of her, she thought it best not to tell them about her run in, so to speak, with the law. There was nothing much to tell anyway. At this point she was as much in the dark as everyone else.

"I thought you said on Friday you were going to stay in this weekend," Stella reminded her.

"I was, but I had too much to do; what with grocery shopping and things," she offered lamely. "You know how it is when you live alone."

"So, you weren't with Luther then?" she persisted with a weird smile plastered on her face.

"No," Raven reiterated. "I just had a lot of errands to catch up on." Hoping this would satisfy Stella's inquisitive nature, she turned back to the large crate in front of her.

She had successfully removed the top and was rummaging through the packing material when

Stella asked avidly, "have you heard the latest?"

"Dish it girlfriend," Charles chimed in.

Assuming Stella was referring to museum gossip, Raven answered distractedly, "yeah. I hear Frank in receiving is…"

"No, not that," Stella interrupted. "I mean about the murder at the University. It was on the news," she murmured watching Raven closely.

"I heard about it," Raven responded dully. No need to tell Stella, she'd heard about it from the police, she decided.

"It's unreal," Stella chortled arrogantly. "That Juanita Ellison is or was as big as a blimp. The whole thing is causing quite a stir on campus." Charles joined Stella's arrogant laughter. He seemed to think if he laughed at what she laughed at he'd score some point with her. Unfortunately, his spastic giggling was no match for Stella's powerful guffaws; so he gained no ground in that arena.

"Come again?" Raven asked with real interest.

"The murder is causing a stir on campus. This is the first time in the school's history that something like this has…"

"No, I mean about Juanita's looks. What do you mean big as a blimp?"

"People are calling her blimp girl," Stella elaborated snidely. "Thunder thighs, expansive gut, a goatee."

"Get out!" Charles snickered.

"A what?" Raven demanded at the same time.

"A goatee", she repeated with a derogatory laugh. "I believe our Ms. Nita had to shave most mornings."

Falling silent, Raven digested the news of Juanita's appearance. This made even less sense, she thought. According to Mac, Luther and Juanita were heavily involved. But if Stella's description of the girl was accurate, then this Juanita person wasn't Luther's type. Why would he sneak around with someone like that? Mac had clearly gotten the facts wrong, because Luther wasn't interested in the Juanitas of the world. If Mac was so wrong about Luther's relationship with the girl; he had to be wrong about everything else, she concluded. Typical policeman tactics, she silently denounced. Trying to pin a murder on the first black man they see and who cares if he's guilty or not.

"Didn't Luther know a Juanita something?" Stella asked with her characteristic ghoulish interest.

"I'm not sure," Raven dismissed with a

nonchalant shrug. "I don't keep track of who's in his life."

"Oh, but I believe he did," Charles offered leaning closer to Stella. "I saw them down on Michigan at the…"

"Don't you need to get back to your department Charles?" Raven asked sharply.

"I can work anywhere there's a computer," he tossed snidely. Offended by her sharp tone, he turned to Stella to confide whatever else he knew about Luther and Juanita quietly. Poor, pitiful twerp, Raven quietly lamented at their chummy stance. Stella will never fall for someone like you.

Running a hand tiredly along the back of her neck, Raven marveled that two days ago, she'd been blissfully unaware of murder and seedy Lawndale apartments. She'd been happily looking forward to the arrival of their latest exhibit. Pouring through crates filled with African art and treasures usually inspired the same euphoria as Christmas. But now, she stared down at the dramatic dance mask in her hand dully. As expected, her text message had kept Luther away from her apartment. She hadn't heard from him since his hurried call, asking her to meet him there. New to the world of subterfuge and intrigue, she wasn't sure if this was a good thing or not. She would ask Mac if no news from Luther was good news. But she suspected he would take sadistic delight in hauling her hiney to the pokey for withholding vital information during an investigation. Sighing, she placed the mask on a nearby table.

"I'm sorry sir but this area is off limits to the public," Stella announced.

"That's right," Charles piped for good measure.

Looking up, Raven spotted Mac striding into the stock room. Trying to pretend she didn't know him, she reached inside the crate and pulled out a small wooden figurine. Examining the wooden figure with rapt absorption, she angled her body towards the light. This effectively put her behind a large pillar and she hoped against hope that Mac hadn't seen her. She knew she was out of luck when she heard Stella voice sternly, "sir!" But Mac ignored her. Instead, he strolled purposely across the room and dropped his arm casually around Raven's shoulder. Raven tensed immediately by the gesture and Stella's gasp of complete disbelief. Mac's arm tightened imperceptibly when Raven tried to inch away.

"What are you doing here?" she hissed from the corner of her mouth.

Leaning down to whisper in her ear he asked, "any news from Luther?"

"No," she softly replied; all the while observing Stella's stunned expression. "Stella…um…this is Mac Reid," she introduced into the awkward silence. As Stella's expression changed from stunned shock to murderous rage, Raven quickly added, "he's…um...Luther's…. uh, he's a friend." Exchanging a, you've got to be kidding me look with Charles; Stella acknowledged Mac's presence with a curt nod. She and Charles leaned forward, making no bones about the fact they were clearly listening to every word of their conversation.

"Is there somewhere we can talk in private?" Mac asked with a pointed look in their direction. Placing the small figurine on the table, Raven led him to the far side of the room.

"What are you doing here?" she demanded when Charles and Stella were no longer within earshot.

"Checking out the museum," he offered with a look of blatant naïveté Raven wasn't buying. "The Field Museum is one of the finest in Chicago," he added enthusiastically. Rolling her eyes at his overplayed enthusiasm, she decided no one in their right mind would mistake him for a natural history enthusiast. He was as big as a football player and coy innocence didn't suit him. Dressed in a dark blue suit and long beige overcoat, his general

53

appearance just screamed police detective.

"How did you know where to find me?" she asked; before realizing it was a stupid question. By this time, he probably knew the brand name of her toothpaste, she thought angrily. "Am I under police surveillance?" she asked, not liking the sound of that at all.

"No," he admitted.

"Then why are you here?"

Why was he there Mac wondered? Other than the fact that he couldn't get her out of his mind, there was no official reason for him to be at the museum. The image of her delectable body displayed to perfection in lavender long johns had resulted in more than one cold shower over the weekend. He would not be able to look upon a pair of long johns as a benign article of clothing ever again, he thought. Watching her shift uncomfortably before him, he noticed, she was dressed simply in off-white khaki slacks and a lightweight green sweater. Even in this attire, she was sexy he decided. The girl would be sexy in a parka, he smiled. Her chocolate body still carried the subtle scent of vanilla and it took all of his self-control not to drag her into his arms for a deep searing kiss. Instead he asked, "what do you do here?"

Surprised by the question, Raven answered truthfully. "I'm a curator. I specialize in West African Art.

"And Stella?"

"My assistant," she answered warily, not wanting to give anything away.

"Who's the squirt?" he nodded at Charles.

"Charles is an accountant here at the museum. He's got a thing for Stella," she offered, anticipating his next question. As they watched, Charles stood abruptly and marched out of the room. Obviously, Stella had just given him his walking papers. Either that or he was zipping home to make her a four course meal.

"These exhibits go all over the country, right?" Mac asked.

"That's right. Sometimes they travel all over the world. This particular exhibit is a traveling one. It came from Mexico."

"From here it will go…"

"Atlanta, I think, but I'll have to check to be sure."

"Were you here when this exhibit arrived?"

"No. But Stella is in charge of receiving the exhibits and making sure the paperwork is in order.

But I can assure you everything is legal and above board," Raven informed him. Not sure where he was going with all these questions about the exhibit she said, "customs would have notified us long before now if there was a problem."

"Pardon me Raven," Stella interrupted. "But there's a call for you about the display case on level B. Want me to take a message?"

"I have to take this," she said to Mac.

Stella glared caustically at Mac as he watched Raven retreating to the other side of the stock room. She bristled with barely contained rage, when she saw his eyes wander slowly across Raven's backside in a lover's caress.

Once Raven was well out of earshot, Stella turned to Mac and blared in a nasty whisper. "Your orders were to stay away from the museum Mac! What the hell are you playing at showing up here now?"

FIVE

"I'm checking out the Natural History museum. Why else would I be here?" Mac replied in a bored tone.

"Hmph!" Stella fumed. She was well aware he was in an area completely off limits to the public. "There's no need for you to be here!" she spat, glowering at him. "I can handle things on this end. You go handle whatever it is you do."

"I would," he derided. "But there is the debacle of Juanita's death. They're looking at it pretty closely at the station. My advice would be to shut down operation until things cool down."

"What am I paying you for!" Leaning towards him aggressively, she sniped, "you were supposed to make it look like an accident!"

AMETHYST HUE

"Hard to do when it was so obviously murder."

"I don't care how you do it; just keep it away from this operation."

"Shutting down for a while could…"

"We're not shutting down," Stella interrupted with an angry hiss. "We're fine where we are. We just need to be careful." Pointing her finger menacingly at his chest, she reminded, "And don't forget you're working for me! I own you!"

"For the moment," Mac agreed casually. But his eyes had hardened to a gritty coldness which belied his casual tone. "What happened to Juanita could just as easily happen to you. So don't push me."

Taken aback by what she read in Mac's cold eyes, Stella sputtered, "I'm just saying there's no need to over react. We've had set backs before."

"Does Raven suspect anything?" Mac asked. As he watched her scribble notes on the phone pad, his features softened with tenderness.

"She doesn't suspect anything," Stella drawled smugly. Following his line of vision, she boasted, "I told you I can handle Raven."

"Like you handled Luther?" he demanded grimly.

"That was a mistake…"

"Obviously," Mac interrupted.

"We'll find him," she spat. "He's bound to get in touch with Raven sooner or later. And when he does…"

"I'll be there to deal with it," Mac announced. "I'll be sticking to Raven like glue from now on," he informed her harshly. "I don't want any more screw up."

"Don't put this on me!" Stella began belligerently. "You're the one who brought Luther into this! I warned you something like this might happen! But oh no," she denounced sarcastically. "The great detective knows everything. Luther should never have been trusted with…"

"Is everything alright?" Raven asked. Caught up in their heated discussion neither had noticed her quiet return. Oh joy she thought, silently bemoaning their angry expressions. She should not have left them alone. Stella was probably giving Mac an earful on her hatred of the white cop.

"Everything's fine," Mac replied stiffly. "I was just telling Stella that you and I would be seeing a lot more of each other." Looking at Stella with a challenging glare, he dared her to contradict him. Not bothering to comment Stella turned angrily and sashayed back to her workbench.

"Sorry about that," Raven felt impelled to say. "But she can be a bit intense about some things."

"I meant what I said," Mac murmured. "You and I will be seeing a lot more of each other." Watching him saunter towards the exit, Raven wasn't sure if he was making a promise or a threat.

{}

Returning to her workbench, Raven stared at Stella expectantly. "Well," she finally voiced into the awkward silence. "What was that about?" The mutinous look on Stella's face told Raven that for once, her normally talkative assistant was not in a confiding mood. But she persisted anyway with, "what's going on with you two?" Snorting inelegantly Stella didn't answer. "Do you know him?" Raven pressed.

"Why would I know a white cop?" Stella demanded belligerently. "He cares this much," she snapped two fingers angrily in the air, "about the plight of the black man. He just wants to harass the…." At this point, Raven zoned out. It was as she'd feared. Stella had gotten worked up and argued with Mac, simply because he was a white policeman. With a resigned look on her face, she wondered for the umpteenth time why Stella carried such animosity for the boys in blue. She'd once tried to coax the information out of her; but Stella clammed up tighter than a tomb guarding a sacred secret, when the conversation was directed towards her personal life.

"Take this little thing with that blimp Juanita," Stella was saying when Raven zoned back in on the conversation.

"You mean her death?" Raven asked sarcastically.

"Yeah," Stella droned distractedly. Continuing as if the death of Juanita was no big deal, she sneered snidely, "wouldn't surprise me if a cop killed her."

As she removed packing material from a nearby crate, Raven asked, "why would a policeman…"

"They don't need a reason!" Stella brayed. "Remember a couple years back when a teenager was gunned down in the back? They thought he had a gun, turns out he didn't." Raven remembered the case all too well. It had practically sent the city spiraling out of control, and dangerously close to the brink of rioting.

"This Juanita business could be the same thing," Stella was saying. "Maybe she knew something, or had something on one of them!"

"Like what?" Raven asked dubiously.

"Could've been anything," Stella answered vaguely. "I bet Ms. Nita was the type to stick her nose in other people's business."

"You got all that from a news report?"

"She just seems the type," Stella murmured as she reached inside her crate again. "I bet she wasn't a student either," she sniped bitterly.

"The news report definitely said she was a student," Raven corrected.

"Hmph!" Stella snorted. "If that girl was a student, then I have a rare tropical bird that lays gold coins. She was a reporter!" she flung at Raven's baffled look. "I think she was pretending to be a student to get the drop on her target. My guess is she stuck her nose where she shouldn't have, and it got her killed."

Watching Stella closely as she carefully removed a bronze statuette from a crate, Raven realized her assistant knew a lot more about Juanita than was natural for a casual observer in a random murder case. Raven had only learned of Juanita's existence a few days ago; yet here Stella sat giving her line and verse on the girl's life.

"How do you know all this about Juanita?" she asked.

"I watch the news," Stella dismissed.

"So do I," Raven pointed out. "Juanita being a reporter wasn't on the news; nor did they show her picture. So just how do you know what she looked like, and how do you know she was a reporter?"

"People talk," Stella answered evasively. "If you'd pay more attention to the gossip in your hood, you'd know all about her too. Anyway, they haven't come right out and said a cop killed her," she quickly amended at Raven's raised eyebrow of skepticism. "But they have certainly implied a suspiciously high level of police involvement.

"The news exaggerates Stella. You know that."

"What better way for a cop to cover his tracks," she uttered. "Let's say for argument sake a reporter got wind of a crooked cop," she offered as a plausible scenario. "In this case, all he'd have to do is get rid of the undercover reporter; then presto change-o he finds the nearest black man to pin it on."

"I guess," Raven murmured not convinced.

"You guess!" Stella challenged. "What part of the theory don't you get?" But before Raven could reply she said, "the police will be looking to pin this murder on a black man. And before you can say halleluiah, a brother will be charged with the crime."

Observing her assistant askew, Raven asked, "do you really think something like that would happen in this day and age Stella?"

Recognizing she was going over the top in her accusations, Stella laughed self-consciously and replied, "I'm just saying Chicago has a history of crooked cops trying to reach an arrest quota, that's all. And if you were smart," she emphasized looking at Raven keenly. "You'd stay away from Mac. He's not someone I'd trust any further than I could throw him."

{}

Sitting on a park bench quietly unpacking her lunch; Raven was too fried to appreciate the scenic beauty around her. The gazebo and sunlight dappling through multi-colored leaves didn't even register. Nibbling idly on a carrot stick, she leaned back and inhaled deeply. What a day, she silently breathed. Stella had harped on Mac and the police department all morning, insinuating they were somehow involved in Juanita's death. She'd offered no real evidence to support her theory; operating under the assumption that the policemen involved in the case were white; and Juanita was black. According to the logic of Stella, this naturally made the policemen crooked and Juanita an inept reporter sticking her nose where it did not belong.

Taking a long draught from her soda, Raven considered her assistant's behavior with new eyes. Stella, always a little weird, was giving way too much emotional attention to a case she wasn't directly involved in. And no matter what she said to the contrary, her animosity towards Mac had to be personal. Frowning in concentration, Raven wondered if Stella and Mac were secret lovers. She dismissed the idea as ludicrous, given Stella's take on the white policeman and his need to oppress the black man. But then again, Stella was not prejudiced. Her relationship with Charles was a testament to that.

Her anger towards Mac could be an act. Pretending anger and animosity towards someone you're deeply attracted to, was not unheard of. Homophobes did that on a daily basis. The thought that Stella and Mac could be secret lovers jarred on her senses for some reason. It's not that she found Mac attractive, Raven quickly rationalized. He was free to date whomever he wanted. But still, she admitted, she didn't like the idea of him being romantically linked to anyone. But before she could dwell further on such troubling thoughts she was galvanized into action.

Out of nowhere a speeding car jumped the sidewalk and lurched right at her. Her lunch went flying and she barely had time to clear the bench, before landing awkwardly against the gazebo. Badly shaken, she watched the careening car race out of the park. It hadn't even slowed after trying to mow her down in broad daylight. With her heart beating rapidly in her chest; she let out a violent scream and leapt away from the gazebo, when Mac suddenly appeared from his crouched position. Tripping over her feet, Raven landed with a cumbersome thud on the ground. She would have glared at Mac for scaring her, if she had not felt like a complete nincompoop in her awkward position.

"Are you alright?" he asked watching the speeding car with narrowed eyes.

"I think so," Raven responded. Trying not to show how creeped out she was by his sudden appearance, she ungainly got to her feet. She thought he'd left the museum grounds hours ago. Had he been hiding in the gazebo this whole time, she wondered? The man clearly had issues, she silently decreed.

"Did you see the driver?"

"No. It happened too fast," she replied.

"It was probably a drunk driver," Mac explained. However, Raven got the impression, he didn't believe that any more than she did. The car had jumped the sidewalk and came straight at her.

"I need to sit down," she uttered sinking onto the nearest stone bench. Taking a steadying breath, she asked, "What are you doing here? I thought you left hours ago."

"Waiting for you," he replied.

"And that doesn't sound creepy or suspicious at all," Raven breathed under her breath.

But Mac heard her and his lips tilted upwards in a slight smile. "Everyone knows you lunch out here on a regular basis, don't they?"

"Yes," she answered slowly. "But that doesn't explain how you knew to wait for me here."

"I'm a cop. I'm paid to know these things," he replied evasively.

With her creep factor already on high alert, she looked at him with narrowed eyes and asked; "are you also paid to be sneaky and stealthy, or are you just following me?"

"Hardly," he grinned. "I have a team of people for that." At her horrified expression, he grinned broadly and said, "chill Raven. I'm teasing you." When she continued to eye him warily, he admitted, "Gary has been known to frequent Grant Park. I was hoping to catch him here." Nodding understanding at this explanation, she visibly relaxed. "While we're looking into Juanita's death and how it may connect to Luther's disappearance, it might be best if you broke from routine. Shake things up a bit," Mac advised solicitously.

"Because of Gary?" Raven scoffed. "I'm not afraid of Gary."

"Gary may very well have friends who drive speeding cars."

"Then it wasn't a drunk driver?" Raven voiced. Alarmed by the implications of his suggestion, she said, "someone connected to Gary is out to get me?"

"Hard to say at this point," Mac responded soothingly. "But just in case, it's best to break with routine."

"Dang it," Raven uttered, "I knew I should have brought my gun with me."

"You own a gun?" he asked surprised.

"And a permit to carry concealed so don't start with me."

"Why do you own a gun?"

"My parents thought Chicago was too reckless and dangerous for me to be on my own. It was either a piece, or have my father move in with me. I chose to pack."

"Have you fired this gun, like ever?"

"Yes, many times. So don't make me shoot you," Raven advised.

"Right," Mac smirked. Obviously, he did not believe she owned a gun, Raven noted. "If you're not up to going back to work after an ordeal like this, I can take you home," he offered.

"Shouldn't we call the police?"

"I am the police," he reminded with a brief smile. "We'll collect your things, and I'll file the report on this reckless driver." he promised.

"Alright," she accepted falling in step beside him.

Truth be told, Raven felt safer with Mac at her side. But even so, she couldn't help casting surreptitious glances around the park for another careening car as they made their way back to the museum. When a car innocently made a right turn, she scampered closer to Mac and did not demur when he put his arm protectively around her shoulders.

Stella was racing up the hall looking harassed when they reached Raven's office. Surprised to find her assistant in such an agitated state, Raven asked, "what's going on Stella?"

"Raven," she uttered a little too loudly. "My computer crashed. I was just finishing up this paperwork on the exhibit. I was hoping to use your computer?"

"Sure, fine," Raven responded distractedly. Approaching her desk, she collected her purse and prepared to leave with Mac.

Catching her arm as she moved to go past him, Mac rumbled softly, "I want a quick word with Stella. Wait for me outside the museum Raven. I'll be there shortly."

"Um," she nodded pushing through her office door.

The look Mac turned on Stella once Raven left the office was so menacing, that Stella immediately backed away from the desk.

"I wasn't trying to hurt her," she informed him baldly.

"Really!" Mac snapped harshly. "Because from where I was standing it looked like you were trying to kill her."

"Well I wasn't. I was only trying to scare her. I thought if she was scared, she'd contact Luther."

"That's assuming she knows where he is."

"Of course, she does!" Stella squawked. "Luther's running scared. If he's going to contact anyone it will be his sister. And before you get all high and mighty," she added at the gathering storm on his countenance. "Just remember Raven may be the only leverage we have to use against him. We need to…"

"Make another move on her," Mac snarled; "and finding Luther will be the least of your worries."

"Are you threatening me?" Stella demanded. Despite her truculent stance, she was intimidated by his belligerent behavior and she backed further from the desk.

"No, I'm giving you an iron clad promise."

"There are people on the food chain higher than me Mac. They want this cleaned up. I'm under a lot of pressure to…"

"Increase the body count," he offered with venom. "I told you before, leave Raven to me. I'll find out where Luther is."

SIX

Watching his car disappear down the street, Raven decided Mac was acting weird; or weirder, she derided. One minute he was all attentive about the near hit and run; the next minute, he was like a block of ice with barely discernable speech patterns. He had rejected all of her overtures to enter into polite conversation on the short drive to her apartment; and his obvious desire to escape her company, had her practically doing a tuck-n-roll leap from his car. He had peeled away from the curb when she barely had both feet on the sidewalk. Clearly something had happened with Stella. Entering her apartment, she tossed her keys on the counter before locking and bolting the door. Then for good measure, she attached the security chain. Whatever was going on, she'd have to get the low down from Stella. Mac was clearly in his *I'm-a-policeman-and-I-don't-discuss-police-cases-with-civilian's* mode. Despite the fact that said civilian was nearly mowed down just minutes ago.

"The chump," Raven fumed. "I could've been killed for all he seemed to care!"

Getting a bottled water from the fridge, she groaning inwardly at her ringing phone. The caller ID told her it was the one person she did not wish to speak to right now. Emitting an audible sigh, she answered the call.

"Hello mother," she enthused with false gaiety."

"Raven are you alright?"

"Luther!" she squeaked surprised. "Why are you calling from Gurnee? Please tell me mom is not a part of this."

"She's not."

"Then why are you calling from her phone?"

"It's complicated."

"Illegal activities usually are," she replied.

"What makes you think...?"

"I did not spring forth fully formed from a rock last Tuesday," Raven interjected in some frustration. "Luther a girl is dead, you're in hiding; and I was almost run down by a car at work today."

"I don't suppose it would do any good to ask you to stay out of this now?" he finally murmured.

"Nope" she agreed. "Besides your associates think I know what's going on; what with the near fatal experience with a speeding car," she mouthed sarcastically. "And let's not forget you called me remember. You dragged me into this by sending me to that broken down shack of a building in Lawndale. Now are you going to tell me what's going on?"

"Nope," he mimicked her earlier reply.

"Fine!" Raven spat in frustration.

"I should never have gotten you involved. I just want…."

"Fine whatever," she mouthed. Irritated he was now trying to shut her out she asked, "but if you didn't want my help, why did you call?"

"I was hoping to find Mac with you?"

"What!" she asked in stunned disbelief. Jiggling the phone cord to insure she'd heard him correctly, she asked, "Not the police detective Mac Reid?"

"Uh…yeah…" he replied shyly. "I…uh…think maybe he can help."

"Help!" she said as if Luther had suddenly gone bonkers. "Mac is a policeman. You think he's okay?" she asked. She was perplexed by the ever changing role Mac was playing. Was he hunting Luther down to turn him in, or was he helping him?

"I think we can trust him," he answered with a shrug in his voice.

"We?'

"I asked him to keep an eye on you?"

"What!" Raven nearly exploded.

"He'll watch out for you, so please stay close to him."

"I can take care of myself."

"I don't want you hurt Raven. Untangling you from this mess is my first priority. Mac can help."

The anxiety she heard in his voice had her grudgingly accepting, "ok," she said. "But how am I supposed to get in touch with him?"

"Don't worry about that," Luther assured her. "He'll find you. He's good at his job Raven."

"I just bet he is," she mouthed doubtfully.

"Raven will you give him a shot? I have too much on my plate to worry about you right now."

"Alright already; don't have a cow," she said under her breath. But she needn't have bothered lowering her voice, because she was talking to the dial tone. Replacing the receiver, she paced her apartment reviewing her conversation with Luther. He hadn't given her any new insights about the case. In fact, he hadn't said much of anything except to tell her to butt out.

"Sorry I sent you to Lawndale ole girl; now stay out of my life," she muttered sarcastically. Going into her bedroom, she changed out of her work clothes into a pair of jeans and running sneakers. Calling Ash, she filled her in on the weekend's events.

"Luther is what?" she sputtered scandalized.

"He's missing but…."

"Wait…" Ash interrupted her explanation. "You did say murder, right?"

"That's right. I need your help looking…"

"Oh no; no flipping way!" she blurted. "You're not dragging me, a law abiding citizen, into one of your law breaking schemes."

"I'm not asking you to do anything illegal Ash. I just want to take a look at a building," Raven hedged.

"Uh huh," was her skeptic reply. "What about the police?" she asked.

"I'm working with the police," Raven assured her.

"Fine," she agreed. "But if this goes south, I'm outa there Raven."

"Agreed," Raven allowed. "Meet me in ten minutes." Giving Ash the address, she snatched up her car keys and left her apartment.

{}

Raven had positioned herself strategically across the street from Juanita's brownstone. She was waiting for her backup, to arrive. A quick glance at her watch told her Ash was late as usual. The girl would be late for her own funeral, Raven predicted, as she watched the building intently. The brownstone looked surprisingly mundane, she thought with a wry twist of her lips. She had been expecting more haunted mansion and less Norman Rockwell. The tree lined street was almost a post card image of the lighter side of Chicago. It was hard to imagine a body had been found there. Shuddering at the thought that someone had died inside the brownstone, Raven gave herself a mental shake and hunkered in. She would make her move as soon as backup arrived, she decided.

"Did you find a good spot?" Raven murmured sensing Ash approach.

"I parked right behind you," she answered as she knelt beside Raven.

"Good we need to…. good googly-moogly Ash!" Raven gasped softly when she turned to look at her. "What is that on your face?"

"Football grease," she whispered back. "Football players use it all the time to reflect sunlight glare."

"They only put a strip under each eye; you have it smeared all over your face."

"I'm incognito for the heist."

Rolling her eyes, Raven rose from her crouched position. She was trying to appear nonchalant and casual. But with Ash dressed in black running shoes, black sweats and a black hoodie they were bound to draw too much attention. The football grease smeared heavily across her face didn't help matters. She looked like she was about to rip off the nearest gas station.

"Will you please take that off?" Raven asked handing her a tissue. "And why are you dressed for a bank robbery?"

Ash began to wipe the grease from her face while observing activity across the street. "Uh... Isn't that police tape on the door over there?" she asked. Surreptitiously scanning the street to see if anyone was giving them any undue attention, Raven quickly nodded yes. "Then we are about to break the law?"

"No, we are about to look at a vacant apartment."

"An apartment with crime tape on the door?"

"If we act natural like we belong here, we should be ok. If anybody asks, we're looking to move into the area," Raven suggested.

"Right, what's our next move?"

"Act casual," Raven instructed. "Not that casual!" she immediately hissed when Ash slithered to the ground impersonating a wino. Helping her to her feet, Raven heaved, "ok... we're going in." Turning they darted across the street and raced up the steps to Juanita's brownstone.

"Now what?" Ash whispered.

Raven was reaching for the door handle when a loud bang was emitted from the other side. With a startled scream, Ash turned and raced down the steps. She didn't stop running until she reached her car. Jumping in, she was about to take off when she noticed Raven waving for her to stop. Opening the passenger door, she wheezed, "either get in or stay out. I'm outa here Raven!"

"Worse.... backup.... ever...." Raven heaved as she angled into the car. "It was just a little noise."

"Is someone back there?" Ash puffed.

"You mean like the disembodied soul of Juanita, dragging the lifeless corpse of her latest victim behind her?" Raven chuckled. But noticing Ash's white knuckled grip on the steering wheel, she swiveled in her seat to search the deserted street. "We seem to be alone."

"Whew," Ash heaved reducing her speed. "What just happened?"

"Er...you heard a noise, screamed like a little girl with pigtails and made a wild sprint to your car." Raven murmured. "In broad daylight."

"I told you if this thing went south I was outa there," she replied sheepishly.

"I didn't think you meant that literally."

"Someone was inside," Ash voiced. "I thought you said the place would be empty."

"It should have been. Someone obviously had the same idea we did."

"Breaking and entering?"

"We didn't actually break or enter anything Ash. We barely touched..."

"Only because someone beat us to it," she exclaimed. "We're not cops or investigators Raven," she stressed. "You're a curator in a museum and I'm in design. We have no business snooping around a dead chick's apartment."

"I just want to get an idea of what's going on with Luther," she replied.

"Let the police do that," she directed. "Look Raven, I told you on the phone if this got hairy I was out. I'm having heart palpitations..."

"Fine wimp-etta," Raven interrupted. "Drop me here on Michigan; the station's just down the road."

"What about your car?" Ash asked pulling to the side of the road.

"Once I make my statement to Mac I'll have him drop me off."

"Ooooh its Mac now," she snickered.

"Grow up will you," Raven advised. "He's just the detective working the case."

"When can I meet this Mac?" she simpered.

"It's not like that," Raven derided her sophomoric behavior. Exiting the car, she assured Ash there was nothing between her and Mac.

"What-evs," Ash replied before pulling away from the curb.

SEVEN

Raven was only a few yards from the police station when someone stepped in front of her.

"You got a dollar so I can get home?"

Raven did a double take at the woman's appearance. She was tall and reed thin; with walnut brown skin and hair that looked like it had been electrocuted. It was sticking atop her head, going in every direction except down. She was wearing a colorful eye patch over her right eye and pushing a shopping cart with her bony hands. Raven handed over the dollar and tried to mosey on her way.

"You got another dollar so I can get fries and a coke?" the woman asked angling her cart in front of Raven."

"No, I don't," Raven responded and went around the cart. She had just reached the steps of the police station when she felt a soft thump on her back. Turning she saw the woman had hit her. She had actually balled her scrawny hand into a fist and struck her. A bold move, Raven thought. Considering how one good shove would reduce the woman to a rickety pile of degenerate bones. The lady had to be in her sixties and looked very malnourished.

When the woman angled her cart towards her Raven stumbled backwards and tripped over the steps. She was down in an instant.

"Crud!" she muttered under her breath. "I so don't need this right now." Wondering if she could claim self-defense for taking out a homeless old lady, Raven struggled to a seated position.

"You going in there?" the woman cackled.

"Planning on it," Raven replied.

"I wouldn't," she shrugged as if they were discussing the price of meats at the meat market.

If I had a tendency to hit people, then I wouldn't go in either Raven silently thought. Aloud she said, "I have police business."

"You reporting me?" she asked lifting her

eye patch to glare at Raven with both eyes.

"Do I need to?"

"You got a smart mouth for a sissy girl," she cackled revealing grungy yellow teeth. The door to the station open and the woman looked up startled. Turning quickly, she disappeared down the street.

Raven sat staring after her bemused and a little confused. Without warning, she was lifted in one strong swoop to her feet. Turning to thank her rescuer, she was pleasantly surprised by the detective helping her. His thick black hair was neatly styled, and his intelligent eyes flicked back to her often as he talked on his cell phone. His approximate two hundred pounds set very well on his muscular 6'5 frame. His physical race was difficult to decipher. He had brown skin, moss green eyes and dimpled cheeks. The overall effect was dramatic and stunning. He was also at the epitome of physical condition, she observed trying not to openly drool.

Ending his call with, "I'll get right on that," he turned to give her his full attention. "I see you met Sadie," he smiled. "AKA the cat lady," he added relaxing against the railing. Raven noticed distractedly that when he leaned back against the railing, his shirt pulled tightly across his broad chest emphasizing his flat abdomen.

"She's crazy," Raven said because it seemed some sort of response, other than licking his lips, was called for.

"That's the general consensus," he agreed.

"Why isn't she under arrest or something?" Raven asked.

"Because no one will press charges against her," he replied. "People get squeamish about sending someone that old up the river."

"I can relate," Raven shrugged. She would have a hard time pressing charges against the old bat herself, she mused.

"Bradford Hobart," he introduced extending his hand. "But call me Brad; everyone does."

"Raven Jahoda!" she yelped when she was shoved unceremoniously from behind. Falling into his arms, Brad moved her behind him protectively. His large body effectively shielded her from the angry bulbous nosed woman being led into the station. The woman glared at Raven hatefully as if she was somehow responsible for her being in handcuffs. Her scantily clad body left little to the imagination; and Raven had no trouble deducing her profession. "It was good you came out when you did," Raven replied when the woman was safely inside the station.

"Uh, we were watching from the window," Brad nodded.

Looking up Raven saw several policemen grinning broadly at them. "Aw man," she cringed. "How much did you see?"

"All of it," he replied unable to douse the mirth lingering in his eyes.

"Great," she sighed with an air of acute embarrassment. The only consolation was that Mac had not been a witness to her moment of public humiliation. Clearing her throat, she said, "I'm looking for detective Mac Reid."

"He's out, but maybe I can help."

"Someone tried to run me over at work today."

"Any idea who?" he countered.

"No. But it might have been a drunk driver," she offered hesitantly.

"You don't believe that?" he asked, taking note of her skeptical expression.

"Lunchtime seems a bit early in the day to be that drunk." Not to mention the car jumped the sidewalk and came straight at me she silently added.

"So, you're saying this was done on purpose?"

"Yes."

"Did you get the license?"

"Nope."

"Did you see the driver?"

"Nada," Raven said shaking her head.

"Anyone with a grudge against you?"

"The cat lady. She wants another dollar."

Smiling Brad asked, "Anyone else?"

"Not that I know of."

"I'll see that Mac gets this information," he responded handing her his card.

"C. Bradford Hobart," Raven read. "What does the C stand for?"

"Christopher," he grimaced. "You want a black kid beat up in the hood name him Christopher."

"It could be worse," she commiserated. "It

could be Susan."

Laughing Brad said, "If you have any questions about anything give me a call."

Raven had a bazillion questions. But now that she was at the station, she was too embarrassed to tell him, she'd gotten spooked when trying to investigate Juanita's place; so she'd sprinted to the station like a spineless sissy to find Mac. Staring into Brad's warm intelligent eyes, Raven felt like a complete idiot.

"Wait a minute... er... Jahoda right?" he asked flipping through his notes. "I thought your name sounded familiar. You look like your brother."

"Actually, he looks like me," Raven corrected. "I'm the oldest."

"Sorry I stand corrected," he smiled. "I know Mac is the lead on your brother's case, but I looked at it briefly. Seems to me that the timeline is off; and your brother had a clean record prior to all this."

"Thank you," Raven said relieved. "That's what I've been trying to drill into Mac's thick head."

Chuckling softly, Brad admitted, "he can be

single minded, but he is a good cop."

"Any way," she murmured feeling vindicated by Brad's supportive attitude, "that's all I wanted to say to Mac. Luther is a good kid. He doesn't break the law."

As she was leaving he asked casually, "you haven't heard from him since he disappeared have you?"

"Not really," she responded. "But I stopped by Juanita's place on my way here." In a conspirator's whisper, she confided, "I went up to the door, heard a noise and ran."

Brad threw back his head and laughed. His laughter was infectious and Raven found herself chuckling softly. "Any hoo," she stressed when he began to rein in his laughter. "I left my car there and I was hoping you could give me a lift." Her admission sent Brad on another round of laughter.

{}

Plunking down on the sofa Raven stared at the Chicago skyline. She was losing it, she decided. She was slowly but surely slipping into insanity. What had possessed her to go to Juanita's place? Even if she had gotten inside, she would not have known what to look for. Rubbing her temples tiredly, she wondered what Luther was up to now? It certainly didn't help her mood that he was warning her to back off; or that she had run from Juanita's place like a certifiable sissy.

What now, she grimaced darkly, at the thunderous knocking on her door? If she encountered one more skeleton from Luther's closet, just one more; she was going to lose it, she bleakly predicted. Looking through the peep-hole, she saw Mac with his face partially obscured by the brown bag he was carrying. Good lord, she silently heaved. She was in no mood for another grilling session on the whereabouts of her brother. Nor was she in the mood to look at evidence, she decided. Glowering at the brown bag resentfully, she unlocked the door.

"Look!" she began belligerently as soon as the door was open. "Just how many times do I have to tell you I don't know where Luther is? I haven't seen him in weeks so…"

"And good evening to you too," Mac smiled; as he shouldered his way into her small foyer. He was wearing jeans and a Chicago Bears sweatshirt. Raven thought he looked windswept and casual. "Kitchen to the right?" he tossed, heading in that direction. It was only then she noticed the brown bag was not an evidence bag because it was full of groceries.

"What are you doing?" she demanded trailing anxiously behind his retreating back.

"Starting dinner," he shrugged as if they dined together on a regular basis. Sitting the bag on the counter, he began to rummage through her cupboards.

"You can't just barge in here and make yourself at…"

"Where do you keep your skillet?" he asked looking up from his stooped position. "I also need your chopping board, rice steamer and mallet."

"This is insane," Raven heaved in frustration. Making no move to locate the items in question, she asked suspiciously, "why are you really here?"

"To fix us a warm nourishing meal," he replied. "It's getting cold out there," he jerked towards the window. "We could both do with some nourishment."

"But…"

"But nothing," he smiled taking in her tired anxious eyes. "You look like death."

"Excuse me!" she sputtered completely thrown by the casual insult.

"You-look-like-death," he enunciated slowly. "You'll never make it to the end of this investigation at this rate. You need to calm down," he soothed as if her world had not been tipped off its axis since he came into her life.

"I should be wired and on edge!" she argued. Angered by his soothing demeanor, she uttered, "I'm not used to criminal activity and intrigue. This is my first case."

"I know," he agreed in that same calm irritatingly soothing voice. "But that's no reason to skip lunch or dinner. You need looking after," he said locating her skillet and placing it on the stovetop.

"How do you know I skipped lunch?"

"It splattered all over the sidewalk if I recall," he reminded. "And your record breaking sprint across three city blocks had to work up an appetite," he grinned.

"What do you mean!" she thundered. "You've been watch…" About to go off on a tangent, she stopped abruptly. Luther had asked him to watch out for her, she remembered. His call earlier had been for that very purpose. Oh no, she thought sarcastically. He hadn't called to check up on her; or to see how she was handling the mess he'd thrown her way. No, he called to see if Mac was on the job as guardian extraordinaire. Stewing silently, she tried to grapple with the fact that whatever was going on, Mac and Luther were obviously in cahoots.

"Is Luther a drug dealer?" Raven asked baldly.

"No," Mac replied with a guarded look on his face.

Sweet, she silently fumed at his shuttered expression! Not only was Luther shutting her out; but apparently so was his partner in crime. She felt extreme irritation that for all their closeness as brother and sister, Mac clearly knew more about Luther's private life than she did. Feeling her temper rise, she glared at Mac resentfully. His mere presence was giving her a headache. As he maneuvered efficiently around her tiny kitchen she snapped, "Luther told me you'd come."

Resisting the urge to rub her temples tiredly, she tried to focus on Mac's movements as he deftly prepared dinner. "Apparently, Luther's hired you to watch out for me," she voiced sarcastically.

Looking up from the macadamia nuts he was expertly chopping he asked, "and that bothers you?"

Shrugging her shoulders, she said, "it's hard being kept in the dark. Not knowing what I'm up against is actually more stressful."

He could tell that, Mac silently acknowledged as he examined her wilting figure expertly. For all that she was trying to hide it with a false show of anger; she was showing signs of stress. Her shoulders were drooping and he would guess she had a rousing headache. "You look like you could do with a drink," he informed her reaching for the bottle of wine he'd brought with him.

"I don't drink," Raven replied dully.

"A massage then," he countered coming around the counter towards her.

"No!" she snapped stepping back

"A warm relaxing soak to ease your stress and tension," he advised in that soothing tone that was starting to grate unbearably on her nerves.

"Stop trying to mother me," she uttered acidly.

"Hey I'm on the clock here," he grinned disarmingly. "I can't have you flipping out my first night on the job."

"I'm not going to flip out. I'm just saying I've earned the right to know what's going on, seeing as how someone tried to run me over with a car," she voiced with irrefutable logic.

Gazing at her for several long moments, he finally conceded, "you're right. While you're soaking, I'll fix dinner. After dinner, we'll discuss the facts of the case."

"Right," she agreed feeling her spirits rise. She was finally getting some answers.

Turning to go, she was stopped in her tracks when Mac murmured, "and you can tell me all about your trip to the station."

"You know," she cringed taking in his suppressed laughter.

"About your street fight with the cat lady? Yeah I know." He said grinning broadly. "You had a fight with a little old lady."

"It wasn't a fight. It was a misunderstanding."

"I heard she decked you and you went

down."

"For the love of…" Raven heaved rolling her eyes heavenward. "I tripped on the steps. She didn't knock me down."

"Oh, if you say so," he voiced skeptically.

"For the record," she pointed out. "I don't go around knocking down old ladies."

"Good to know," he nodded. "Now about this cat lady beat down…."

"Cook your stupid dinner," she interrupted. Leaving the kitchen, she made her way to the bathroom for a warm soak.

EIGHT

With a sigh of contentment, Raven slid deeper into the vanilla scented bubble bath. She'd been luxuriating in the tub for nearly thirty minutes, and was in no hurry to get out. The heated foamy water had performed its magic and she felt as limp as a piece of cooked spaghetti. She could hear Mac moving around in the kitchen as he prepared dinner. The delicious smells seeping through the bathroom door, told her he wasn't all talk. The man knew his way around a kitchen. But who was he really, she wondered? And how did he connect to Luther?

The soft knock on the door had her looking towards it expectantly. "Dinner in ten minutes," was muffled through the closed door.

"I'm coming," Raven murmured. Reaching

for a fluffy towel, she was draping it securely around her wet body when Mac opened the door.

"What did you say?" he began. His voice rumbled to a halt as his eyes roved hungrily over her body. Her brown skin against the fluffy white towel was intoxicating. The water beading across her back and shoulders was...

"What?" Raven demanded. Turning to find him staring at her intently, she asked, "did you lose something?"

"I didn't realize you were so short," he quickly improvised.

"I'm not," Raven corrected. "I identify with tall people."

"Why?" he smirked. "You're short."

"Your face is short," Raven muttered as she shoved past him.

"Wow," Mac grinned clutching his chest dramatically. "That was a real zinger." Trailing her to her bedroom, he said, "I don't know if I'll ever recover from that third grade insult."

"Shut up."

"Said it once and I'll say it again," he

purred. "You have height issues."

"Whatever," she shrugged.

"Have you tried a twelve-step program?" he innocently suggested. "I hear they can work wonders with people of your height. They're starting a new class at the Y if…"

"Listen gigantor!" Raven suddenly blared. "You need to get over your obsession with my height. Just because you're abnormally tall, doesn't mean the rest of us are short."

"If you say so shorty McShort Short."

Rolling her eyes in frustration, she heaved, "I'm not having this conversation with you Mac; besides I need to get dressed."

"Go ahead," he encouraged. Leaning comfortably against the door jamb, his slumberous eyes gazed at her with longing. "You're not bothering me," he husked.

"Out!" Raven ordered. Shooing him from her bedroom, she slammed and locked the door.

"Dinner in five minutes," was uttered from the other side.

{}

Raven entered the kitchen to find the delicious
smells permeating the air were more pronounced.
Her growling stomach told her, she was more than
ready for a good square meal.

Turning from the stove, Mac saw she had
changed into a pair of peach long johns. Only this
time, they were discretely covered by a white knee
length robe. Her hair was held away from her face
with a peach ribbon, but left to cascade to her
shoulders. As desire flooded his system, he thought,
she was unbearably sexy. The peach color made
her brown skin glow; and he only had to recall how
long johns encased her body like a second skin, to
send his desire into overdrive. Long johns had to be
the sexiest attire in her repertoire, he decided.
Allowing her to see his blatant desire, he gave her a
lazy smile.

Raven felt her stomach muscles tighten in
response to his smile. His darkening umber eyes
were nearly her undoing. She released her breath
slowly when he turned to place the finishing
touches to the table. With his back to her, she made
a detailed inventory of his physique. He had an
athlete's body, she determined. Broad muscular
back, strong arms, and a really nice derriere, she

smiled unconsciously.

"Raven?" he rumbled.

With a start, she realized Mac was holding out her dinner chair invitingly. Clearly embarrassed, she asked awkwardly, "so…uh…what'd you make?"

"Coconut chicken," he answered taking mercy on her discomfiture.

"Uh, is that…?"

"Indian cuisine," he enlightened. "Turmeric, ginger and cumin form the basis of the dish."

"It smells like curry."

"Turmeric, ginger and cumin are the basis for curry. In India, the spice curry doesn't exist. Curry is a western concoction to take the guess work out of spicing Indian cuisine.

"It smells delicious."

"Hope you like spicy." he replied spooning rice on his plate.

"Love, love, love spicy food," she assured him. Taking a cautious bite, she exclaimed, "this is great! Where did you learn to cook like this?"

"The navy," he murmured in the middle of swallowing.

"You were in the navy?" she asked surprised.

"I was a Seal," he commented nonchalantly.

Gazing at him critically, Raven thought he definitely had the physique of a navy Seal; but he just seemed too....

"Too what?" he queried causing Raven to stare at him surprised. "My specialty was reading people," he explained. "And you don't exactly have a poker face."

"Well stop it," she shrugged. "It's creepy that you can do that."

The conversation continued along innocent lines for the remainder of the meal. Mac was a charming and attentive dinner companion and Raven found herself listening to his antidotes with rapt attention. She responded naturally to his bantering and light flirtation and accepted his help amicably with clearing the table and loading the dish washer. She'd completely forgotten the sinister nature behind his visit and was jarred back to reality when he said smoothly, "let's review the case by the fireplace. Now I have Bavarian wild berry or lemon ginger herbal tea," he announced digging inside the grocery bag again. "Which do you prefer?"

"Wild berry," she murmured. Moving towards the sofa, she felt the tension, she'd lost in the last two hours, returning with a vengeance. She needed to hear what he had to say, she chided. If things were bad, they were bad. No sense ducking the truth. Whatever Luther was up to, it was best to get it on the table and deal with it properly. It probably wasn't as bad as she was thinking anyway, she surmised. Besides, every cloud has its silver lining, she thought inanely. "What?" she asked in response to Mac's soft chortle.

"Nothing really," he smiled good naturedly. "It's just that you've squared your shoulders and have such a stoic expression on your face; like you're getting ready to face the gas chamber or something."

"I do not."

"If you say so," he commented. Carrying two steaming cups of herbal tea towards the sofa, he joked, "and I'm sure you're not mentally reciting platitudes; like if life gives you lemons make lemonade."

"Shut up," she voiced crossly, refusing to

admit she was doing just that.

Patting the sofa next to him, he looked at her invitingly. Sitting down beside him, she stared woodenly at the fire. "Well?" she uttered when he didn't immediately begin his gripping narrative.

"Comfy?"

"I'm fine."

"Cause I could get you a pillow."

"I'm fine. Quit stalling."

Gazing at her averted profile somberly, he softly asked, "how much do you know about what's going on with Luther?"

"Not much," Raven admitted reaching for her tea. To hide the fact that his close proximity was making it hard not to focus on his very kissable lip, she took a cautious sip. "I work fulltime at the museum and Luther attends college. We don't run in the same circles."

"Then you don't know what he does off campus?"

"Not really."

"Umm," he murmured while Raven took another nervous sip of tea. A loaded silence fell;

with Raven waiting tensely for him to proceed. He remained silent for so long, she finally turned to look at him. "I hate to be the one to tell you this," he said watching her closely. "But this is about drugs."

{}

"What!" Raven sputtered completely shocked at having her suspicions confirmed. I mean it was one thing to suspect drugs were involved, she reasoned. But to have it confirmed in no uncertain terms was another story. "I thought you said Luther was not a drug dealer!" she voiced trying to remain calm.

"He's not," Mac supplied feeling her stiffen at his side.

"He's using?"

"No," Mac replied. Choosing his words carefully he soothed, "Luther's helping me out of a situation…"

"What situation?" Raven interrupted highly agitated. "He's not on the police force!" Waving her arm wildly to indicate the ever lurking presence of the police, she screeched, "you have a squadron of policemen who can help you out! Why do you need a college student?"

"Calm down," Mac advised. Rescuing her tea before it spilled onto the sofa, he set is gingerly on the side table. "The plan was simple enough. Luther was to pose as a runner on campus."

"A runner?"

"Someone who can move drugs around campus. His cover was perfect. He had access to a lab and his lab partner was a known user. We were tracking how the contraband was getting on campus. In order to get to the man at the top we needed someone on the inside," he said. Lifting the hand, she hadn't realized was fisted at her side, he massaged it gently. "The FBI was brought in to contain…"

"Aren't you a cop?"

"I'm FBI," he replied flipping out his badge. "The FBI was brought in when it became apparent this operation spanned several states and Mexico."

"So how does Luther fit into all this?"

"He's a grad student who's planning a career in forensic science with the FBI. He wanted to do some field work."

"Field work!" Raven denounced. "This isn't field work! Field work would be looking for microscopic evidence. It's not being the scapegoat for the FBI."

"He's not a scapegoat, and I can assure you his involvement was completely voluntary. We needed a student who already had a connection to the drug world. Luther's linked to a user. Gary," he explained at her searching look. Observing that she appeared calmer, he retrieved her tea from the side table.

Nursing the wild berry tea absently Raven found the delicious aroma and rich berry flavor surprisingly soothing. Attempting to digest what Mac had told her thus far; she took several calming swallows. Staring deeply into the amber liquid, she asked, "so what happened to Juanita?"

"I'm afraid she was Luther's mistake."

"He killed her?" Raven asked with horrified eyes.

"No," Mac quickly soothed drawing her to his side. When Raven instinctively snuggled into him, he draped his arm possessively around her waist. Laying her head heavily on his shoulder, she gazed with slumberous eyes at the fire. She found the leaping flames mesmerizing; and the occasional crackle from the ceramic logs relaxing. In fact, she was suddenly finding it hard to concentrate and was straining to focus on the conversation at hand. "Juanita was a reporter. She was itching to break the story, before we had sufficient evidence to make a conviction hold up in court. How she managed to sway Luther to bring her in, is anybody's guess. She was caught recording a drop and was taken out."

Yawning widely Raven asked, "don't tell me you think Lu…"

"Luther's not a killer," Mac interrupted.

"Then who took Juanita out?"

"That we do not know," he supplied. "It's possible Luther may know. He was in pretty deep and got fairly close to the target."

"Who's the target?" she murmured trying to stifle another yawn.

"The night Luther made contact with the target was also the night he disappeared. We were to rendezvous at our safe house at midnight and he was a no show."

"Um," Raven mumbled sleepily.

"They've already killed once and won't hesitate to kill again. Luther isn't safe as long as he's out there. And you're not safe now that they've connected you to him. They may try again to flush him out by hurting you. That hit and run at the museum was their way of putting him on notice," he said.

"What?" Raven yawned.

"Letting Luther know they will hurt you if they have to," he informed Raven's inert form. Smiling indulgently at her faint snore, he removed the now empty tea cup from her hand.

Cradling her gently in his arms, he held onto her as if he never wanted to let her go. Raven was proving to be more of a distraction than he needed right now.

NINE

Raven snuggling deeper into his chest had Mac rethinking his decision to let her fall asleep in his arms. The effect on his anatomy from her warm body, had him clinching his jaw in frustration. The situation with Luther could not have come at a worse time. If Raven found out how close he was to her brother's disappearance, she might not understand. He wished he could tell her more about the case; but for her own safety, he had been purposely vague. The slight vibration from his cell phone, had him extricating Raven's sleeping form from his tall frame. Laying her gently on the sofa, he flicked open his phone. Scowling at the name appearing in the caller ID, he pressed the answer button.

"Reid," he barked harshly into the receiver.

"Well?" Stella barked right back.

"Well what?" he derided moving towards the window. Glaring at the twinkling city lights, he knew without her even asking, what she wanted.

"Where are you?" she demanded.

"I'm with Raven."

"Can you talk?" she asked stiltedly.

"She's asleep."

"Asleep?" Stella queried suspiciously. "Who sleeps at eight o'clock?"

"I slipped her a sedative during dinner."

Laughing nastily, she gloated, "I knew you'd find a way to distract her."

"She's no good to us neurotic Stella. She's wound so tight right now, she could stroke out. The sedative will insure she gets a good night's sleep."

"Whatever," Stella denounced disdainfully. "Did she tell you anything?"

"She doesn't know anything."

"Don't be fooled by that helpless act of hers," Stella sneered. "Luther pulled the same thing which is why…"

"I know innate paranoia comes with the business we're in," Mac interrupted caustically. "But this is a bit over the top even for you."

"My paranoia has kept us one step ahead of the law," she informed him.

"It has its place," Mac agreed gazing at Raven curled seductively on the sofa. "But getting worked up over someone as harmless as Raven."

"Harmless!" Stella screeched scathingly. "She was at the police station today. Who knows what she told them! If the police find Luther before we do we're finished! And you needn't think you'll come out of this smelling like a rose. You're in this just as deep as I am, so don't forget that!" she warned.

"If Raven knows anything, I'll get it out of her."

"How?"

"I told her I was FBI."

"She bought that old trick," Stella spat flippantly.

"She did," Mac responded.

"Did you also tell her that Luther and Gary were cooking meth in the chem lab; that he'd started a side business of his own? Hell!" she spat; "If he hadn't gone missing, we would have taken him out."

"I thought it best to leave that part out," Mac responded.

"But what if the police have him? What if he's in a safe house? He could be spilling his guts to the Feds as we speak."

"He's not," Mac voiced gratingly. "But if Raven knows anything she'll tell me."

"That could take weeks," Stella argued. "If she knows anything we need to get it out of her now. I don't like this Mac. I don't like it!"

"She's starting to trust me."

"We're wasting time. We need to move on this Mac."

"Haven't you learned by now Stella, that you can catch more flies with honey than vinegar?" he asked.

"I don't like this," she defended her desire to move things along. "What if she said something to the police?"

"She didn't."

"How can you be sure?"

"She would have told me if she had."

"Why?"

"Because Luther called earlier to tell her I'd look after her," he divulged. "Only she wasn't talking to Luther. She was talking to me."

"You?" Stella squeaked dubiously.

"That's right," Mac responded in Luther's voice. He remembered how irritated Stella had been when he'd taken the time to learn the timber and infections of Luther's voice.

"So, what if it was," she derided. Not willing to admit his parlor trick; as she called it, would help them out of the mess they were in, she sniped, "that trick of yours won't help much now."

"I believe it can," he replied.

"How?" she demanded.

"For starters, I will be watching out for her. Now that she thinks I'm FBI, she will confide in me. She won't be making anymore unannounced treks to the station."

"Good one."

"I can be very persuasive when I want something Stella," he reminded in a seductive whisper. "You of all people should know that."

"Raven will see right through your phony charm," she predicted caustically.

"You didn't," he reminded her smugly. At her angry intake of breath, he continued, "let me do what I do best Stella. Raven believes I'm here to help. She'll confide whatever she learns about Luther to me."

"But what if Luther…"

"I told you earlier. I'm not leaving Raven's side. I don't want any more screw ups. Juanita's death could have been avoided."

"Don't take that noble attitude with me," she simpered. "Our little Raven would be surprised as hell to know how closely connected you are to Juanita's…"

"Goodbye Stella!" Mac cut her off harshly. Snapping his phone shut, he glared out the window. Running a tired hand along his stiff neck, he thought the case seemed to be complicating itself. Returning to the sofa, he gazed down at Raven's sleeping form. Lifting her effortlessly, he carried her through to the bedroom. Settling her under the warm comforter, he bestowed a chaste kiss on her forehead. In the living room he doused the lights and sank into an armchair. Placing his holstered gun on a nearby table, he stared broodingly at the flickering fire.

{}

Stretching fluidly, Raven surfaced to the smell of bacon wafting through her bedroom door. Completely relaxed, she stretched again with a wide yawn. She'd slept surprisingly well, considering the high level of anxiety she was under. She could hear Mac tinkering around in the kitchen, and her heart raced in anticipation at seeing him again. Grabbing a robe, she headed for the bathroom to complete her daily ablution.

Showering quickly, she returned to her bedroom to dress. Deciding against the casual thrown together look she usually wore when involved in cataloging a new exhibit; she chose her outfit with care. Selecting a pair of black pants and pink cashmere sweater, she skillfully applied makeup, before painting her full lips a rich cherry red. Running her fingers deftly through her thick hair, she left it to fall loosely around her shoulders.

Exiting the bedroom; she found Mac in the kitchen, humming snatches of various pop songs. Pulling out a chair, she sat down. Like the night before, he had set out a delicious spread. Bacon, hash browns, eggs and toast. I could definitely get used to this, she thought in appreciation.

"Hey sleepy head, I was just about to come wake you," he grinned from the kitchen doorway. Looking up, she saw the look of desire which seemed to be permanently etched on his face when looking her way. Even as she watched, his eyes heated to a fiery glow of desperate need as they roved possessively over her torso. "You look great," he finally husked.

"Thank you, so do you," she offered taking in his brown denim pants and casual sweater. "Don't you have to work today?"

"I'll be on campus most of the day," he responded as he sat the coffee decanter on the table. Taking a seat himself, he said, "We're still trying to track Juanita's last movements. We're hoping someone on campus may have seen or heard something."

"What do you want me to do?" she asked spooning eggs on her plate.

Although asked with benign curiosity, the husk

in her voice caused his male anatomy to jerk in his jeans, as his imagination ran riot. What would she do, he wondered; if he told her exactly what he wanted her to do to him right here and now? Shifting to ease the discomfort in his jeans, he groaned, "I want you…"

"Yes?" Raven interrupted looking up with startled anticipation.

"To go to work as usual," he finished.

"Oh," she uttered clearing her throat. "I could help on campus."

"True," he agreed downing a mouthful of hash browns. "Or you could blow my cover. One word from Gary and it's all over. He knows you're Luther's sister."

"Doesn't he know you're undercover with Luther?"

"Nope and he's not going to," he countered. Pouring them both orange juice, he said, "for an undercover operation to work, no one involved in the case can know your true identity. Which means you can't tell anyone who I am."

"I wasn't planning to."

"Not the police, your family, friends or even

119

Stella," he stressed.

"Stella?" she quipped surprised. "Why would I tell her?"

"I got the impression the other day the two of you were close."

"Not at all," Raven denied shaking her head. "We work together, but we don't hang out. She does her thing and I do mine."

"She seems rather intense," he observed leaning casually back in his chair.

"And that was a good day," Raven laughed. "She can get downright mean, belligerent and nasty."

"I'll keep that in mind," he said feeding her a slice of bacon. Thrown by the gesture, Raven momentarily lost her train of thought. She shuddered slightly when his fingers gently brushed her lips. His caressing smile told her, he was just as enraptured with her touch, as she was with his.

In an attempt to collect her scattering wits, she took several sips of orange juice. Mac tracking her every movement with seductive eyes was not helping with her composure issues, she thought with chagrin. But with a Herculean effort, she managed to pull herself together to utter, "this is my brother we're talking about so I want to do something to help out Mac. Sitting around idly waiting for news to trickle in will…."

"Sitting around idly will keep you safe," he advised. "And I want you safe," he murmured gazing at her affectionately.

"You do?"

"You know it."

"Well okay then," she smiled. "I'll concede to your wishes this time."

"And next time?"

"We'll see," she purred.

TEN

Sitting at her desk pondering the morning events, Raven unconsciously doodled all over her inventory sheet. Mac had already taken up residence in her subconscious, she admitted. But he was starting to live large in her conscious thoughts as well. She might as well admit she found the guy attractive. Those warm umber eyes and massive arms. Plus, a killer smile that could dazzle...grinning, she scribbled over her doodle when realizing she was unconsciously drawing Mac. She could get used to waking and finding him in her apartment, she sighed; especially if he was going to make breakfast.

Giving herself a mental shake, she looked down at her inventory copy. The words blurred into meaningless dribble as she recalled how Mac had first alarmed her with his news about Luther; then surprised her with the news that he was under cover for the FBI. She should have known, she realized. Mac's entire persona pretty much screamed good guy. Besides, she grinned ruefully, he was spending way too much time in her daydreams to be a murdering psychopath.

"What's gotten into you?" Stella snapped. Annoyed Raven seemed to be in la-la land, she tossed the invoice in question on her desk. With a frown of disgust, she practically glared at Raven.

"Nothing," Raven replied picking up the invoice to skim its contents. Not liking that of late, Stella had taken to dogging her steps and questioning her every move; she asked, "what's your problem Stella? Lately you've been crabbier than usual."

"Man trouble," she answered with a display of feminine camaraderie that was clearly forced.

"You and Charles had a fight?" she asked.

"It's not Charles," she derided with an irritated shrug.

"The two of you are always together. I didn't know you were seeing anyone else," Raven voiced surprised.

"I'm not now," she admitted sourly. "He

was a big dumb loser."

"Ok," Raven remarked not knowing what else to say. She knew perfectly well Stella was not into girl talk or commiserating over her monthly cycle. This sudden need of hers to open up was a bit disconcerting. Initialing the invoice, she handed it back to her.

Taking the invoice from Raven's outstretched hand, Stella asked abruptly, "are you seeing anyone?" But before Raven could answer she said, "I thought you were taking things slow since your break up with Derek."

"That was nearly two years ago," Raven reminded her with a careless shrug.

"Yeah, but it was a bad break up."

"That it was," Raven agreed.

"So, what's up?" she gushed with a fake show of gaiety. Looking Raven up and down, she said, "something's up with you. What's going on?"

"Nothing," Raven murmured; but silently acknowledged, she might have taken extra care with her appearance because of Mac. When Stella continued to eye her critically she said, "I just wanted to try something new."

"We're in the middle of cataloging the new exhibit!" she denounced eyeing Raven's pink cashmere sweater caustically. Although she had her hair pulled back in a ponytail, her subtle make-up and red lipstick resulted in a striking picture. She looked business chic, Stella observed.

"Apparently looking pretty is not just for the weekend," Raven replied with a nod in her direction. With the sun hitting the copper highlights in her hair, Stella looked positively radiant, she silently allowed. Well she would Raven amended, if not for the dark scowl marring her pretty face.

"You're looking more than just pretty and you know it!" Stella glowered. "You never dress us just to catalogue an exhibit. And you never wear make-up either."

"Like I said," Raven intoned, "I wanted to try something new."

"No doubt it's all for Mac's benefit!" she sneered.

"Excuse me!" Raven demanded. She did not like the attitude Stella was displaying in her office. The girl was her assistant after all, not the other way around.

Realizing her mistake, Stella mouthed woodenly, "sorry. I just don't want to see you get hurt again. After Derek…" she trailed off.

As apologies went, it was fairly lame Raven thought. But Stella was one of those people who'd rather face the throes of death, than apologize for anything. So as lame as it was, it was something coming from her. Nodding slightly to let her know her apology was duly noted, Raven asked, "why should I get hurt?"

"Mac!" Stella uttered in frustration. "You're sleeping with him, aren't you?"

"No, I'm not."

"He was at your place last night," she uttered belligerently.

"Was he?" Raven asked distantly.

"I'm betting," she spat. "Based on your attire and stupid expression I'm betting you got some last night."

"And that concerns you how?" Raven asked. Gazing at her assistant critically, she voiced sternly, "you are aware my personal business is none of yours."

"I'm just saying you shouldn't mess around

with a guy like Mac."

"Why do you care one way or the other, Stella?"

Snorting inelegantly, Stella didn't answer. She merely offered an off handed shrug as if she could care less.

"Just this once Stella, I'm going to feed your sick obsession with my life and point out that Mac and I are just friends."

"Is that the current euphemism for the nasty?" she hmphed.

"Think what you want, but it's the truth."

"He's a white cop!" Stella bellowed. Clearly miffed that Raven did not see Mac in the same heinous light that she did; she continued outraged, "he's just another slimy, sleazy control freak trying to bring down the black man. The police force is riddled with them."

"Uh huh," Raven murmured unconvinced.

"If you ask me, he's just playing at being a cop anyway," she threw into the charged silence.

"How so?"

"Reid! Of the Macauley-Reids!" she

announced as if that explained everything. At Raven's baffled look, she voiced emphatically, "the Macauley-Reids are one of the riches families in Chicago."

"Never heard of them," Raven admitted.

"That's cause they're old money. They own most of Hyde Park and a portion of Lincoln Park," she ticked off two of the riches neighborhoods in Chicago. "They also own land on the waterfront in Cleveland, two restaurants here in Chicago, a ballpark; they're building that new mall in…"

"So, Mac doesn't have to be a policeman?" Raven observed. She sensed Stella could give her a run down on every asset he owned. She was also feeling somewhat embarrassed, she'd immediately assumed his opulent home in Lincoln Park was the results of bribes and kickbacks.

"Oh yes he does," she snorted snidely. "The way I hear it his family cut him off." At Raven's look of real interest, she elaborated, "there was some scandal about a drug addict cousin. Apparently, Mac got the boy on the stuff and the boy tried to fly without a plane. Now he's a cripple. Mac has been black listed by the family ever since. I hear they didn't leave him two nickels to rub together."

"Are you mad that he's a cop or are you mad that he doesn't fight for his inheritance?" Raven wondered.

Angrily whacking a nearby file cabinet in frustration, Stella glared at Raven. "Girl use your brain," she challenged. "Why would a man with his connections not fight to keep the family jewels? His cut alone has to run into the millions. Instead he chooses to give up a life of luxury to run around the back alleys of Chicago; why?"

Shrugging mystified Raven offered, "maybe he wants to help clean up the city. You know make it a safer…"

"And maybe I have blue eyes Gandhi," Stella interrupted irritably. "He's a dirty cop!" she scowled as if goaded beyond endurance by Raven's bemused look."

"Oh well if that's all," Raven commented casually. "I should have made him pay for using the shower this morning. Now that I know he's rolling in it on the down low I'll have to…"

"Ha…ha very funny," Stella voiced sarcastically. "I'm just letting you know the man's no good. He wouldn't do something for nothing. His so-called help will end up costing you something."

"I'll take my chances."

"He'll use you then toss you aside."

"I'm a big girl. I'll risk it."

"I'm telling you, he's only hanging around because he's trying to use you," she predicted harshly. "I don't think he's into brown skin."

"How do you know?"

"How do you think?"

Aha, Raven silently thought, we're finally getting to the gist of Stella's anger towards Mac. "Interesting how he's not into brown skin, yet according to you; I somehow managed to get some last night."

"Hmph," she snorted loudly.

"I thought your reaction to meeting him the other day was over the top even for you. So how long have you known Mac?" she asked.

But now it was Stella who turned on the mute button, and chose that moment to clam up. "Whatever," she finally mumbled at Raven's quizzical gaze. "Just be careful around him." Turning abruptly, she flounced out of the office.

{}

"What's our next move?" Raven asked as she slid into a booth at *The Deli.* Like most days, the restaurant was packed to capacity. Raven liked the Deli because it was only a short walk from the museum; and the food was great. Today, lunch was on Mac so that made it even better.

"We painstakingly review the evidence we've collected so far," he said joining her in the booth.

"Oh god, that sounds so boring," she uttered with an exaggerated yawn.

"Detective work can be very tedious. That's why…"

"Raven… Raven Jahoda?" was brayed from across the room.

Looking around the crowded restaurant, Raven spotted the culprit immediately. Mainly because she was waving frantically as she made her way through the crowd.

"Oh no," Raven whispered to Mac. "It's my

cousin, Carmelita."

"So?" he murmured watching the woman approach.

"You don't understand. She'll tell the entire family about you."

"So?" he queried again.

"You're sitting too close to me," she pointed out. "We need to have a professional distance between us."

Instead Mac draped his arm firmly around her waist to drag her unyielding body to his side. Carmelita's eyes widened in speculation when she finally made it to their booth. "I thought that was you," she gushed giving Mac the once over.

"I eat here all the time," Raven said.

"I'm Carmelita, Raven's cuz. Carm to family and friends," she introduced. Squeezing into the booth, she cozied up to Mac with relish. "Who's this?" she asked Raven, nodding in Mac's direction.

"Mac Reid," he supplied.

"How do you know Raven?" she asked Mac.

"Raven and I are dating," he announced

gleefully.

"We are not!" Raven denied hotly.

"If you say so dear," he droned in a pseudo hen pecked voice. Massaging her shoulder with the pad of this thumb, he said, "but at breakfast this morning..."

"Breakfast!" Carmelita interrupted with real interest.

"It's not what you think," Raven tried to interject.

But ignoring her, Carmelita turned to Mac and said, "I'm glad to see she's finally dating again. She hasn't been out on a real date since Derek."

"Derek?" Mac probed. Pretending not to notice Raven's attempts to squash the conversation, he encouraged Carmelita to continue.

"Handsome black man of tomorrow," she readily informed him. "He claimed to be a staunch supporter of the conservative right and moral majority. Strait laced to his toes," she added rolling her eyes. "So much so that two years ago, he ran off with Raven's college roommate, Godzilla."

"Gwen," Raven corrected.

But Carmelita was on a roll and she
continued as if Raven hadn't spoken. "Godzilla and
the fool are now living large somewhere in
Indiana," she scoffed. "You can never trust anyone
that strait laced. Mark my words, it's the quiet ones
you have to watch out for," she knowingly decreed.

"Give it a rest Carm!" Raven hurled into
their chummy confiding session. "You've been
harping on the breakup for a while now."

"I'm just saying," she replied. "So, Mac,"
she simpered leaning across the table. "Are you one
of those strait laced quiet types?"

"I'm no boy's scout," he admitted with a
wolfish grin in Raven's direction.

"Good," Carmelita approved. "I think you
might be just what the doctor ordered."

"It's taken a while, but I'm finally getting
through the barriers she's erected around her heart."
Rolling her eyes at this outrageous comment, Raven
was sorely tempted to belt him one.

"I'm just glad to see she's dating again."

"We're hanging out," Raven corrected.

"If you say so," Carmelita soothed patting
her on the hand. Clearly not believing a word of her

protest, she grinned broadly. "Well I don't want to intrude. I'd better get back to my table. It was nice meeting you Mac," she beamed.

"The pleasure was mine," he replied.

When Carmelita was out of earshot Raven hissed, "thanks a lot Mac for misleading my cousin."

"Don't know what you mean," he intoned innocently.

"Don't give me that," she nearly screeched. "You're supposed to be good at reading.... You did that on purpose," she gaped as comprehension dawned."

"Who, me?"

"Why do you want my family to think we're a couple?"

"Because you don't have a poker face. Keeping them busy with questions about your love life will prevent them from looking too closely at Luther."

"But that won't last forever."

"I don't need forever. I just need a little time to solve this."

"What if my parents call? Do I tell them about you and Luther?"

"No, the less people know the better. Trust me; they won't ask," he assured at her skeptical look. "They'll be too busy grilling you on the new man in your life and the beautiful babies we're trying to make."

"Not funny Mac. I'll try and get with Carm later to do some damage control."

"Too late," he smiled nodding in Carmelita's direction. Even from across the room, it was obvious she was giving someone the stats on their relationship. The quick glances in their direction as she cupped her cell eagerly to her ear, were testament to that reality.

"Thank you, Mac. I can expect an urgent call from my Mom and the wedding planner the second this hits the family grapevine."

"Who's Derek?"

"None of your business."

"But your family approved of him?"

"As a matter of fact, they did," she grudgingly replied.

"Did you love him?"

Sighing at his persistence, she asked, "is this conversation really necessary Mac?"

"I'm trying to get to know you; the real you," he forestalled when she was about to voice objections.

"Talking about exes is never a pleasant conversation," she stalled. "Besides, what you see of me is what you get."

Look, I know you're 5'3…"

"5'4," she insisted.

But continuing as if she hadn't spoken, he said, "I know you look damn sexy in long johns and work at the Field Museum. But I'd like to know you the woman. Your likes and dislikes; your dos and won't do," he husked.

Choosing to ignore his suggestive innuendo, she said, "Derek and I met in Philly. I was an archeology student. He was a political science student. Long story short, we fell for each other. He met my friends and family. I met his. We got engaged. He started sleeping with my roommate and we broke things off. End of story."

"He hurt you?"

"Everyone hurts someone," she responded succinctly.

"Now Derek and his bride live an idyllic life in Indiana?'

"I don't know how idyllic life can be in Indiana; but that's where they are last I heard. What?" she asked of his intense look.

"Do you keep tabs on where they are?"

"No," she dismissed. "I know they're in Indiana because Carm and everyone else seem to think I need to be kept abreast of Derek's every move. They seem to think Gwen is just a passing fling since Derek has yet to marry the girl."

"If she is just a passing fling, would you take him back?"

"Hell no!" Raven voiced emphatically.

"Good," Mac rumbled deep in his chest.

"Good?" she asked eyeing him suspiciously. The smirk on his face told her he was up to something.

"What better way to let family and friend know you are over Derek than to introduce them to the new man in your life? I'm betting Carm is spreading the news on the family grapevine that you are seeing someone new right now."

Knowing Carmelita, Raven knew Mac would win that bet.

ELEVEN

Walking briskly back to the museum, Raven had her head bent against the wind. She was rehashing the details of a surprisingly warm lunch with Mac. Once Carm left and her disastrous breakup was cannon fodder on the table; Mac had become a very charming and attentive lunch date. Caught up in her musings, she did not notice Gary sneaking up behind her. He was clinging to the tree line as if afraid of being seen. His shrunken frame was almost completely lost in the oversized coat he was wearing; so much so, that it looked like an animated coat was stealthily marking her movements.

When he suddenly sprung up beside her, she started violently. "Good lord Gary!" she exclaimed.

Trying to maintain her composure, she said, "don't sneak up on me like that!" His appearance had changed drastically since their last encounter, she noticed. In June when he attended a family bar-be-que, he'd been a picture of health and vitality. Now, he was shrunken and shriveled as if he was in the throes of a major illness. His normally tanned skin was pale, and his sparkling blue eyes had lost their glow. He was also nervous and twitchy and couldn't seem to focus his bloodshot eyes.

"Where's Luther?" he twitched reaching for her arm in a jerky agitated manner.

"I don't know Gary," Raven responded flinching out of reach. "I thought maybe he was with you," she probed.

But he didn't take the bait; he just asked more aggressively, "where's Luther!"

"Again, I don't know," she snapped. She was getting sick and tired of everyone assuming she had Luther in her back pocket. She wasn't in on his little scheme; nor had she known about his nefarious life on the side. Till Mac informed her otherwise, she'd believed her brother was a grad student studying forensic science. She figured he dated, hung out with friends and obeyed the law. Now it seemed he had a secret life that clearly operated outside the law.

Screwing his eyes to mere slits, Gary tried to focus on her face. Lunging for her, he sputtered, "I want Luther!"

"Get off me!" Raven cried shoving him forcefully away. Stunned when he collapsed into a helpless heap on the sidewalk, she realized he was little more than a bag of bones. With his coat sleeve displaced, she saw he had scratched his arm raw in places. Didn't he feel that she wondered alarmed? Taking a close look at him, she noticed his overcoat was hiding a shrunken and disfigured body. He had sores on his neck and a seeping sore on his chest. His teeth were rotting and some were missing. The only explanation for his rapid deterioration and erratic behavior had to be drugs, she deduced. "Gary," she tried to soothe, "why don't we…"

Scowling at her soothing tone, he jumped up and began to pace frantically. "I don't need your help," he sneered. "But you better tell me where Luther is…or else!" he glared at her ominously as if this was supposed to scare her. "The people we work for…"

"We?" Raven asked curiously.

"Me and Luther," he scowled. "I vouched for him. He disappeared with half a million in product. Now it's my butt on the line if we can't find him." Taking her stunned silence as fear, he droned smugly, "stop pretending you don't know…"

"What Gary!" she yelled. Not impressed by his pathetic attempt to intimidate her, she demanded, "what is it that I'm supposed to know?"

Losing his bravado at her aggressive attitude he backed down immediately and whined, "you know where Luther is."

"I don't," she argued. "But even if I did, I wouldn't tell you or the people you work with. The ones who sent you to hassle me," she added sarcastically.

Slumping against a nearby tree he mumbled, "I don't know where Luther is either."

Recognizing that for all of his bluff and bravado, Gary was a man clearly at the end of his rope. Seeking to console him, she murmured, "I Know a policeman. We can talk to him about where Luth…"

"The police!" he interrupted looking terrified. "The police are involved you idiot!" Jerking his coat tightly around him; he began to back away from Raven, as if she was an informant for the vice squad.

"Talk to me Gary. What's going on? What is

Luther into?"

Squinting furtively from side to side, he didn't immediately answer. "Are you wired? Is this a set up?" he finally asked twitching more profusely. "Did Luther cut a deal!" he demanded greatly agitated. "Am I being set up?"

"I'm not wired; this is not a set up, and Luther didn't cut a deal as far as I know," she said reaching towards him.

Leaping back as if he'd been scalded, he screamed, "stay away from me!" Without warning he turned and zig zagged his way into a thick grove of trees.

{}

Pulling into an empty parking spot at the museum, Mac glanced briefly at his watch. Raven should be leaving the museum soon. He hadn't wanted to scare her when he'd boldly informed her that he would be picking her up from work from now on. Fortunately, the *I- promised- Luther- I'd- watch-out-for- you* excuse had worked; and the need to tell her, she was now a target had been abated. He'd learned nothing new on campus. His contacts had dried up with Juanita's death; and the once gregarious student body had closed ranks like clams guarding their most precious stone.

Cutting the engine, he stretched his long legs. Things would be a lot easier if he could convince Raven to keep a low profile. Maybe take a little time off work. But he was starting to realize that like Luther, she had a stubborn streak a mile wide. He was amazed he hadn't realized that before now, he smiled. He'd had her under surveillance long enough. One look at her photo in Luther's wallet was enough for him to know that Raven was someone he'd like to get to know better.

By now he knew she was a creature of habit. She always left the museum precisely at a quarter after five. Generally, she left the building empty handed. Watching her shoulder her way clumsily out of the heavy glass door, he grinned. She was struggling to maintain her grip on a bulky oversized folder. Watching her struggle with her awkward cargo his grin broadened. The wind would occasionally snatch an errant piece of paper out of the grim clutch she had on the folder and whip it around the parking lot. Raven would be forced to chase it down and risk losing more papers as they fluttered dangerously close to the edge of her grip. He probably should get out of the car and help her, he thought with a wide grin. But she looked so darn cute chasing paper he couldn't resist watching the show.

"What's all this?" he asked when she finally scrambled into his car.

"Information on Juanita," she puffed taking a moment to catch her breath. "I *Googled* her and got several hits. Did you know there's a web site already dedicated to honor her memory? And another that's trying to sell her stuff? People are sick," she finished disgustedly.

"You…er…don't think the task force handling the case has already reviewed this information?" he queried having difficulty taking her amateur sleuthing seriously.

"I want to be prepared," Raven murmured distractedly. Searching through her papers, she was trying to find the damning piece of evidence she'd wanted to show him. But with her skirmish with the wind, the evidence in question had managed to lodge itself deep within her stack. Trying to dig it out, she dropped the entire bundle. "Aargh!" she quipped in exasperation when papers spilling everywhere pooled at her feet.

"Need help?" Mac asked making a serious effort not to chuckle out loud.

"No I can manage," she replied bending to shuffle through the stash. "I found some evidence concerning bulbous nose on the web site," she mumbled from her bent position.

"Who?" he choked; and this time there was no hiding the distinctive chuckle in his voice.

"Bulbous nose…. oh, you don't know her," Raven supplied. "Found it!" she exclaimed waving the evidence excitedly before turning to stare at Mac in triumph.

"Who or what is bulbous nose?"

"I met her when I was down at the police station. Well I didn't actually meet her," she explained at his raised eyebrow. "But she was staring at me in a daring and hateful manner. I figured she knew something."

"And?"

"So naturally I pegged her as a suspect."

"On the basis of a look?"

"It wasn't just any look," she defended. "It was daring and…"

"I know," he interrupted, "daring and hateful. But even so, that's not enough to issue an arrest warrant or to convict."

"I know that," Raven scoffed. "That's why I went searching and found this!" she announced excitedly. Handing the paper to Mac, she waited impatiently for him to read the brief report. "Well?" she demanded when his eyes shifted back to her.

"I'm not connecting," he said.

"And you call yourself FBI," she lamented reaching for the article. "It says here, she was arrested the very night Juanita was killed. She was working the corner on the very street Juanita was killed on. She has to know something."

"It also says she described a man fitting Luther's description fleeing the scene," he pointed out. Starting the engine, he pulled out of the parking lot to take the five-minute drive to her apartment.

"I'm thinking she said that under duress," Raven said with conviction. "The police are involved. I bet they're strong arming her. We need to question her as soon as possible."

"Why do you think the police are involved?"

"Gary told me. He was at the museum…."

"You've seen Gary?"

"Oh yeah," she heaved. "He was slinking around the park this afternoon. He was a royal mess and looked like the living dead. I don't know if he's all…"

"Did he talk to you?"

"Of course, he did. What do you think I've been trying to tell you?"

"What did he say?"

"He said he needed to find Luther. The people he works for want Luther. They seem to think I know where he is."

"Come again?"

"His friends in high places are under the erroneous impression that I can locate Luther at a moment's notice."

"Is that all he said?"

"Oh, that Luther disappeared with half a million in product." Caught up in her narrative, she didn't notice Mac tensing at her side. "What's our next move?" she asked.

"Our?" he voiced surprised to find himself with a new partner. Releasing the vice like grip he had on the steering wheel, he shot her a quick glance.

"Should I tail the perp..."

"The perp?" Mac repeated with a rueful shake of his head. "I can see we need to get you off of procedural cop shows. Don't get involved with Gary. I want you to call me if you run into him again or if Luther contacts you alright?"

"I want to help Mac. You know Sitting around waiting for news to trickle in will drive me crazy."

"Short trip," he threw in softly.

"Ha… ha, you're just too funny," she derided. "But I'm trying to be prepared Mac. In case I'm out in the field."

"What field?"

'You know, the crime field

"You're not getting into the crime field," he observed pulling up to her apartment.

"I want to help nab the perp that's gunning for my brother."

"The perp?" he choked with barely contained mirth.

"Fine, the perpetrator," she amended. "I figure it's someone with a grudge."

"And I figure, you've been watching way too much television," he voiced grinning out right. "We definitely need to get you off detective shows, film noir and all murder mysteries for the duration of this case."

"I can help Mac," she insisted. "I do have a background in archeology."

"And if we need someone to carbon date a bone we'll call you," he promised as they entered her apartment.

"I can do more than…" Inhaling deeply, she asked, "what is that delicious smell?"

"Beef stew," Mac offered helping her out of her coat. "I put it in the crock pot before we left this morning."

"You think of everything," she smiled following him to the kitchen.

"A hardy meal for a blustery day," he answered looking inside the pot. "I need to make corn muffins. Can I trust you with the salad?"

"Mais qui mon capitaine," she joked. "And for the record, I happen to be a very good cook."

"Really?" he asked dubiously. Taking in her almost bare cupboards, he stared at her with a raised eyebrow.

"Hey, I cook."

"What can you cook?"

"Stuff," she offered with a slight shrug.

"Like what?"

"Stuff too profound for your baby ears to withstand."

"Takeout," he guessed.

"Funny," she grinned. They worked amicably together preparing dinner and Raven decided to let the subject of her helping on the case drop for now. She just wanted to unwind and enjoy the company of a nice man. Since learning Mac's true identity yesterday; her entire attitude towards him was changing. Unfortunately, her silly heart was several paces ahead of her logical brain so she decided to do a little field work on Mac. "How did you get interested in the FBI?" she casually asked, as she dropped lettuce into the salad spinner. With her back to him, she didn't see him stiffen or his face close up like a steel trap.

"A relative got me interested," he said vaguely.

When nothing more was forth coming, Raven turned to stare at him fully. "You don't like talking about yourself?" she asked not really expecting an answer. His body language and averted face were clear indications he did not like the direction the conversation was heading. His noncommittal shrug told her nothing. If anything, it made her wonder if Stella was right about his family secrets. "Mac?" she queried warily.

Suddenly relaxing, he turned to her with a wide grin. "Try this," he urged steering a forkful of steaming hot beef stew towards her mouth.

"It's too hot," she warned nodding at the steam rising from the stew.

Mac proceeded to blow on the beef in such a provocative manner, that all thoughts of grilling him about his family life simply floated out of her head. "Try it now," he husked.

Leaning forward, she accepted the warm beef stew into her mouth delicately. Chewing cautiously on the succulent meat, she marveled that once again Mac had managed to blend his spices to perfection. Closing her eyes, she relaxed fully against the counter to savor the different flavors and textures on her tongue. "I'm tasting garlic and maybe a hint of allspice," she voiced.

Watching the sheer bliss flit across her face, Mac could feel his body heating in response. "You're spot on about the garlic, but way off about the allspice," he groaned moving to the far side of the counter. He needed to put some distance between them; before he completely lost control and flattened her against the wall to slack his lust.

"You're not going to tell me?" she asked with mock chagrin.

"Maybe," he drawled distractedly when her tongue snaked out to lick droplets of stew from her lips.

"It's great," she enthused. "I want the recipe."

"It'll cost you," he grinned gazing at her affectionately. "This here is a genuine Reid original."

"Don't tell me," Raven laughed. "It came over on the Mayflower, and was handed down from generation to generation preserved in grand pappy's sock drawer."

"Yep," he said joining her in amicable laughter.

"So, what do I have to do to get the recipe out of you?" she asked. "I mean, I don't want it said that I intentionally swiped a Reid original."

"Well now," he considered. "This particular recipe will cost you one kiss…"

"Done!" Raven exclaimed leaning over to peck him on his cheek.

"On the lips," he finished.

"On the lips?" she questioned with an exaggerated scandalized look on her face. "Don't you think that's a tad high for a mere beef stew recipe?"

"An original, blue ribbon, prize winning recipe," he pointed out. "You know how many restaurants I have to beat down annually to keep this recipe from going public?"

"None, nada, nil," she guessed enjoying the easy banter between them.

"Try hundreds," he corrected.

"Even so," Raven shrugged carrying her completed salad to the table. "You're an officer of the law. You can't trade recipes for kisses."

"I'm off the clock right now," he reminded her. "I can tell you this," he paused for dramatic effect. "One of the ingredients is bay."

"Bay?"

"Bay leaf," he rejoined as if even the simplest child would recognize bay leaf when they saw it.

"Um," Raven murmured dragging a step stool across the floor. Standing on it to get a better look inside the bowl he was working on she asked, "what are you making now?"

"Corn muffins."

"It looks like goop," she reported.

"For now," he agreed. "But it will end up being a tasty addition to our meal.

"Mac?" she began hesitantly.

When he turned to look at her with mild concern, she leaned over and plopped one right on his lips. "Hey!" he growled surprised. "I wasn't ready for that!"

"It counts," Raven chortled gleefully. "That's Raven one and Mac zero," she laughed marking an imaginary score board in the air.

"But…"

"It counts," she grinned widely. "As you failed to provide a list of stipulations or provisos for the kiss I was forced to take matters into my own hands. Now about this recipe," she crooned smugly. "I'll need it typed and in its entirety by tomorrow. Say six in the morning."

Amused that she had managed to out maneuver him and beat him at his own game he drawled, "as you wish my Nubian Princess."

"And don't you forget it buster! You'll have to get up pretty early in the morning to pull one over on me."

Mac was starting to think the same thing. Watching her with an affectionate smile when she continued to laugh softly about her one up-man-ship; Mac couldn't help himself. He joined her in her contagious laughter.

"But I am not a vindictive soul," she commented when they were able to rein in their laughter. "Tomorrow night I'll cook something for you."

"Really?" he asked taking another look at her nearly bare cupboards.

"Yes really," she assured him. "What do you like?"

"I have a real soft spot for spaghetti," he replied. "But if that's too complicated," he queried with a raised eyebrow.

"Ha!" Raven scoffed. "Spaghetti it shall be," she promised.

TWELVE

Snuggling under her warm comforter, Raven's sleep was interrupted by some evil fiendish person ripping the covers off her. She was left shivering in the crisp chill of an autumn morning.

"Time to rise and shine," a horribly familiar voice chirped cheerfully.

Opening one eye to scowl at Mac, she spat, "what are you doing? And how did you get into my apartment?" He had left right after dinner last night; so what was he doing standing beside her bed.

"I'm checking out one of Gary's hangouts. I thought you'd like to tag along."

"And my apartment?"

"I swiped the spare key from your bureau," he murmured, as if his thievery was no big deal. "This lead we're checking out...."

"Now!" Raven asked incredulously. Looking at the bedside clock, she screeched, "its three o'clock in the morning. Reaching for the comforter as her body trembled from the cold morning air; she blared, "I have to be at work by ten." But Mac had a firm grip on his end and refused to let it go. "Mac!" she shouted irritated.

"If we get there by four that'll give us five and a half hours before you have to be at work," he reasoned. When Raven refused to budge, but laid there glaring at him resentfully, he simply reached down and plucked her from the bed. He stood her not too steady form on the floor.

"When I wake properly," she promised with conviction, "I'm going to slug you." Chuckling, Mac steered her out of the bedroom. Moments later Raven was standing under the shower while warm water gushed over her. Pondering this new facet of Mac's personality, she decided he had to be deranged. He was obviously a morning person; whereas she detested the very idea of early rising. This was precisely why she had an apartment within walking distance of the museum. She'd given up early mornings when she'd made the transition from

Gurnee to Chicago; and she was not about to let Mac drag her back into a habit she considered archaic, she grumbled silently.

"What's taking so long in there?" he asked from the other side of the shower curtain.

"Mac!" she yelped grabbing at the curtain frantically. Poking her head around the curtain, she glared at him angrily. "Can't I have a little privacy?"

"Sure," he responded lazily. Folding his arms across his chest, he leaned casually against the sink. "I'm just here for a breakfast order."

"Anything's fine! Now get out!" Incensed by his soft chuckle as he sauntered out of the room, Raven was sorely tempted to lob the bar of soap at his skull.

"Dress casually," he directed. "Jeans and running shoes should suffice."

Raven finished her shower in record time. She wanted out of the bathroom; just in case Mac decided to make another unscheduled visit, while she stood naked behind a flimsy curtain. Dressing quickly, she made her way to the table.

"Good morning," he enthused. "Isn't this a beautiful day?"

Grumbling something unintelligible, she took a seat. "A warm breakfast for the autumn chill is just what the doctor ordered," he said.

"You should know," Raven mouthed irritably. Not perturbed in the least by her anti-social attitude, he pushed a large bowl of oatmeal towards her.

"Eat up," he encouraged. "We'll check out this lead before I drop you at work."

"Why do we have to go so early?" she murmured biting into a piece of toast.

"Undercover work is not glamorous and it doesn't sleep," he responded. Pouring her a generous cup of coffee, he said, "we have to work the hours our suspect works. Now with Gary here," he elaborated. "We want to catch him unprepared and unrehearsed. If we wait, his cohorts will have time to fabricate a story."

"Fine, whatever," she mumbled. She didn't care what Gary and his associates were up to at this god forsaken hour. Right now, she wanted nothing more than to lay her head on a cushion for a little shut eye. Looking at Mac blearily across the table, she realized the big galoot knew how tired and groggy she was. He probably picked this god awful hour on purpose; just to put her off trying to help, she surmised.

"Don't you want more involvement in the case?" he asked innocently.

"At three o'clock in the morning, no!" she barked itching to wipe that smug superior look off his face.

"Well you know what they say," he grinned. "Undercover work is ninety percent boredom and stakeouts and only ten percent real action."

"I guess," Raven dismissed.

"Of course, if you want me to handle this lead alone."

"I'm up. I'm coming," she uttered.

"Sure you don't want to rest a bit more; get some…"

"I'm fine!" she snapped. "I'm coming with you. I' wouldn't miss this for the world," she added; stifling a wide yawn.

"Alright then," he smiled at her show of stoicism. "We leave in ten minutes."

{}

Sitting in a parked van outside what appeared to be a condemned building, Raven's heart sank. They'd been sitting there for forty minutes without incident. She couldn't believe this was Gary's haunt. He only had a couple of semesters before he finished pharmaceutical school. How had he gotten so far off the mark that he wound up on skid row, she wondered?

She didn't realize, she'd asked the question out loud till Mac answered. "He was headed for a pharmacy degree, until he got derailed by crystal meth."

"Uh, what do we do now?" she asked.

"We watch, and wait."

"For what?"

"Anything suspicious or out of the ordinary," he responded non-committal.

"Um," she nodded looking down the deserted street. If this was a TV movie, the violin music would be starting just about now, and the tumbleweeds would be released from props to roll with abandon down the street. All sane people were still in bed snoozing. Only a couple of nut jobs were squatting in the back of a derelict junk van, peering out of a smudge encrusted window. It was about as interesting as watching paint dry. "I don't see anything?" Raven voiced after giving the empty street the once over. "Can we go now?"

"We just got here."

"I'm having trouble staying awake just sitting here like this. Can we turn on the police scanner or something?

"No."

"Why not?"

"On a stakeout, we need to concentrate on the target."

Staring from Mac to the empty street, Raven wondered what they were watching for. Perhaps Mac expected the trash can to sprout legs and start walking around. Picking up the binoculars, she turned to scour the deserted street. As she scanned for any sign of movement she whispered dramatically; "there they sat...dot, dot, dot...man and woman communing with..."

"What are you doing?" Mac asked.

"Narrating," Raven offered before resuming her dramatic spiel. "Who knows what lies ahead for our intrepid duo...dot, dot, dot..."

"Dot, dot, dot?" Mac wondered.

"Ellipses. Three dots following a sentence means a pregnant pause will follow; or more information is coming. What?" she asked sensing he was staring at her aghast.

"First, no one narrates on a stake out; and second, you actually know the proper name and use of ellipses."

"I read," she shrugged.

"You are a card carrying, certifiable nerd."

"Your face."

"Spoken like a true nerd," he smirked.

"Don't make me bring up your mother," she threatened.

"As if you could," he challenged calling her bluff.

"She's so fat they're thinking of replacing her with Pluto. They're going to call the new planet Fatty Ann."

"What?"

At his bemused gaze, she explained, "Pluto was demoted to dwarf status. There are only 8 planets in our solar system now. Fatty Ann will be the ninth."

"Egad," he chuckled at his outdated expletive. "No one knows about Pluto; ellipses, ellipses, ellipses, except nerds."

"It's dot, dot, dot you moron."

Suddenly serious, Mac plucked her from her seat and lunged to the floor. "We're blown," he whispered. It was only then Raven heard the unmistakable sound of footsteps. They were approaching fast, and there were at least three sets, maybe more. "Stay down," Mac ordered. Throwing his weight into the door, he took out one assailant when the door hurled open. Raven could see from her crouched position, three more approaching.

She was out of the van in an instant. While Mac fought off two, she took on the third. She blocked his right cross, and double tapped him in the stomach. When he doubled over in distress, she rammed her knee in his nose hearing a sickening crunch. He tried to grab her around the neck, but she twisted out of his grip, and tossed him effortlessly over her shoulder. Stumbling to his feet, her assailant began to limp away. Going after him, Raven was stopped in her tracks when Mac grabbed her by the scruff of her shirt.

"You wanna dial it down a notch Rambo-etta. They're leaving." With narrowed eyes Mac watched as the men darted inside an empty building. Minutes later a car squealed from behind the building and disappeared down the street. During the scuffle, he had gotten a good look at one of his would-be attackers. It seemed Stella was making a play to take him out permanently, he mused. Too bad she hadn't factored in Raven's fighting skills. Gazing in amazement at the amped up woman beside him he asked, "where did you learn to fight like that?"

"Advance self-defense class. I'm an instructor. People always assume that if you're…"

"Short," Mac inserted.

"Female," Raven corrected emphatically. "People assume if you're female you're a pushover. They let their guard down giving you the edge."

Examining her closely, he noticed she didn't have a mark on her. "Remind me not to get on your bad side."

"Shouldn't we go after them?"

"No need. I got a good look at one of them. I won't have much trouble tracking him down."

"But…"

"No buts," he said forestalling her
objections. "I got a squadron of people for this type
of thing, remember?" When Mac took out his cell
to call it in, Raven knew she was being regulated to
the sidelines.

{}

Raven slipped out of the museum on her lunch
break to make a stop at the local market. She had
promised Mac a home cooked meal and he was
getting one. Snagging a shopping cart, she
proceeded first to the spaghetti aisle. Grabbing two
boxes of angel hair pasta, she gave a muffled yelp
when the cat lady turned into the aisle. She was
smoking frantically on a pipe as she gazed
longingly at various items on the shelf. Who did
she think she was with that pipe, Raven
wondered... Harriet Tubman? Trying to move
unobtrusively in the opposite direction; she knew
she was out of luck, when the cat lady made a bee
line in her direction and rammed her cart next to
hers. "Har," she mouthed around her pipe.

"What?"

"I said har," she repeated as if her meaning

was crystal clear. When Raven continued to stare at her with a question on her face, she removed the pipe and said, "Hi."

"Oh hi," Raven replied. "Well I'm on my lunch so I better go," she offered.

"Ooooh, Ms. Hoity-toity got a job," she sneered.

"Well bye," Raven called as she moved her cart past. She should have known her second encounter with the cat lady would be as bad as the first. The hag started following close behind her; banging her cart into her every now and then.

"Oopsy," she cackled the first time it happened. When Raven looked back at her, she offered her a grungy toothed grin. "My bad, I didn't know you were stopping," she cackled when she ran upon Raven's heel causing her to almost lose a shoe.

"Why don't you go ahead of me?" Raven asked waving her forward.

"I'm fine here," she shrugged.

"Ladies is there a problem?" the manager asked appearing at their side. But before Raven could answer, the cat lady turned and high tailed it out of the store.

"I'm glad you came over when you did," Raven said.

"We saw the whole thing on the monitors. We'll ban her from the store; can't have someone like that harassing the customers."

"Does she come in here often?" Raven wondered.

"No this is the first I've seen her."

"Um," Raven murmured moving on. She hoped she was not developing a cat lady nemesis.

{}

Luther's eyes fluttered open. As his eyes adjusted to the dim light, the images before him slowly came into sharp focus. In front of him was a sink with debris strewn all around. Above the sink was a small window. Raising his head, he slumped back at the pain this tiny movement caused. He had a massive headache. Trying to move his limbs he noticed he was tied to a cot. Soft clinking noises had him turning his head. Recognizing his lab partner of three years he rasped, "Gary?"

"Shut up!" Gary shouted. Slamming the glass he was about to drink from sharply on the counter, he glared at Luther resentfully.

"Untie me!" Luther demanded jerking at his bindings.

"You shouldn't have come here," Gary mouthed shaking his head slowly from side to side. "You know you're real stupid Luther!" he blasted angrily. "You had every chance to get out. To go back to normal Joe-guy; and I find you creeping around this place." Jerking his arm agitatedly to indicate their surroundings, he stared at Luther morosely.

"No one gets out Gary. You know that."

Watching Luther struggle against the ropes knotted at his wrist, he hollered, "you can forget about leaving! I've called the boss man, and he'll deal with you!"

"Who did you call?"

"Wait and see," Gary muttered losing his bluster. Taking a seat his eyes darted fearfully around the room. "I didn't sign on for no murder," he announced.

"Untie me Gary. I can help…"

"You're already dead Luther," he sighed mournfully. "They told me to get rid of you."

"You're assigned the job of getting rid of me? We're friends Gary."

Shifting uncomfortably, he whined, "I didn't sign up for no murder. I told them that! I told them!" he hollered with menace. "Why is everyone always trying to get me to do something I don't want to do?" he appealed to Luther.

"You don't have to do anything?"

"It's too late anyway," Gary bemoaned. "They're on the way now to get rid of you. I was supposed to finish the job last night." Alarmed that maybe he'd said too much, Gary reached for his drink and drank it down in one swift gulp.

"Gary…"

"Shut up!" he shouted rising from the chair. "I need to think!"

"Have you considered your options?" Luther wondered. Watching Gary pace worriedly around the room, he knew he only had a small window to try and reason with him.

"What options?" he asked stopping his pace in mid stride.

"You kill me, you go to jail for life…"

"No!" Gary roared. "They said they'd protect..."

"Who'd believe a meth addict was innocent?" Luther asked. "And with your small size and pretty face; you wouldn't last in prison," he replied watching him flinch. "Of course, the other option is you kill me, and then they kill you. It'll be easy to pin my death and Juanita's on you."

"I didn't kill Juanita! I had nothing to do with that!"

"I know that," Luther soothed. "But who's going to believe a meth addict? We can help each other Gary. You want to get out of this alive, don't you?" When he nodded yes Luther demanded, "then untie me!"

"Why don't you do as he says," Mac drawled with deadly quiet from the shadows. "Untie the man."

Mac's voice looming eerily from the shadows alarmed Gary so much that he leaped frightfully against the far wall. Careening awkwardly into the sink, several of the empty whiskey bottles clattered noisily to the floor. "Mac," Gary wheedled, "Luther's awake."

"So it would seem," Mac observed coming

into the light. Gazing down at Luther's inert form he asked, "you alright?"

"What do you care?"

With a barely perceived shrug Mac answered, "I'm spending a lot of time with your sister. I want to be able to answer truthfully should she ask."

"Stay the hell away from my sister!" Luther demanded straining against the ropes. "If you so much as lay a finger…."

"You'll what?" Mac mocked looking pointedly at the ropes restraining him. "What will you do Luther; talk me to death?"

"She's not a part of this," Luther murmured simmering down.

"You made her a part of this the second you lured her to the drop in Lawndale," he reminded brusquely.

"Mac," Luther pleaded with an almost desperate look on his face. "I don't want her hurt."

Observing the desperate need on his face Mac nodded imperceptibly before turning swiftly to growl at Gary. "You know what to do!" he barked. "Finish this!"

THIRTHEEN

With brooding eyes Mac stared at the blood stained cot. Luther had signed on for this, he rationalized. He knew the score. It was Luther who went off script, he reasoned. It was Luther who brought Juanita in and mucked up the works. Had he just followed his lead, none of this would have happened, Mac grimaced. He'd have to tell Raven something of course. But that should be easy, he silently scoffed. He'd lie. He was good at lying. Lying was part of the job, he defended. So why did he feel like a heel when he lied to her? She was getting to him; proving to be more of a distraction then he thought she would be.

"Is he here?" Stella bristled, storming angrily into the room. Flinging the flimsy door so hard it banged against the far wall, she looked menacingly around the cramped space. She'd rushed right over when Mac called; she was hoping the last stage of this nightmare was finally over.

"No," Mac murmured, unperturbed by her attitude. Giving her his full attention, he viewed her angry stance with derision.

"Then why drag me down here?" she screeched. "I don't like this Mac," she fretted before he could answer. "We can't have Luther running around like this so close to deadline," she accused.

Mac's nostrils flared briefly at the cryptic insinuation that it was his fault Luther was still a threat. If she wasn't so caught up with saving her own skin, she might realize Luther wasn't their biggest problem. Watching her intently, he said, "then you can rest easy."

"You got him?" she asked with elation. At his curt nod, she flicked open her cell phone and punched in a number. Waiting for the caller to pick up she observed Mac with disdain. "It's about time you did something right!" she derided. When her caller picked up, her entire persona changed. Turning her back on Mac she reported, "we got him and there'll be no more hiccups." She listened briefly before responding with, "a shipment is ready for next week." Snapping her phone shut, she turned to glare at Mac. "It's a good thing you finally took care of Luther."

"I didn't," he responded casually. "Gary's handling it."

"Gary!" she mouthed looking suddenly afraid. "He can't handle a toddler! We're too close to deadline for anymore screw ups!"

"Maybe you should call them back and tell them that," he mocked nodding towards her phone.

Looking at the metallic phone still clutched in her hand, she immediately dropped it in her handbag. She was starting to feel the rumblings of real fear. "I already told them it was a go," she whispered. "They're already mad about…" Looking at Mac with venom she shouted, "I won't go down for this! If Gary screws this up it's on you!" Startled, Stella sputtered incoherently when Mac lunged forwarded knocking her into the wall. Her bag when flying as she bellowed, "get off me you big ox!"

"Next time you send your goons to take me out; make sure they're better fighters!" he snarled.

Gulping Stella stammered, "M Mac. I, I wasn't, I d d didn't…"

"I recognized Troy," he derided. "And yes, he's in police custody," he advised moving to retrieve her bag.

Snatching the bag from his outstretched hand, Stella glared at him in frustration. "How are you still alive!" she spat.

"My guess is Troy will cut a deal and give you up," Mac offered smugly.

"You're an idiot!" Stalking towards the door, she barged through it without a backwards glance. If she had bothered to look back, she would have noticed Mac had her cell phone. He was scrolling through her call list for the last number she had dialed.

{}

"If this isn't a good time we can always do this later," Raven said in response to the silent driven stranger beside her. Hoping to lighten his mood, she teased, "I'm glad you let me off the hook about the home cooked meal. I ran into the cat lady at lunch and she totally put me off cooking tonight." But Mac didn't respond to her light bantering. If anything, he stiffened even more as he drove down the dark road. They were heading for a sports bar-n-grill on the lake. It was a casual establishment, so they were both in jeans and Bears T-shirts. Raven was learning fast that Mac was a complete sport's fanatic; while she was content with just hearing the score on the nightly news. But he had been in a strange mood since he picked her up. He was tense, drawn and basically not in a dating frame of mind. "Did something happen with the case?" she finally voiced, perplexed by his brooding silence.

"It took an unexpected turn," he grudgingly admitted.

"Bad?"

"Bad," he nodded tightening his vice like grip on the steering wheel.

"I'm sorry," Raven murmured leaning towards him to place her hand gently on his knee. Feeling him jerk violently in response, she swiftly withdrew her hand. As if in agony, Mac groaned low in his throat before pulling onto the shoulder of the road. Cutting the engine, he pulled Raven fully into his arms for a deeply searing kiss. Crushing her lips beneath his, he supped on her tongue like a man taking his first drink. "Mac," she panted when he finally let her up for air.

"I need you, to trust me Raven." Leaving a

trail of hot kisses across her neck he husked, "No matter what happens, you have to trust me."

"I do," she gasped. "Mac what's this about?" But instead of answering he captured her lips in another searing kiss. Sprawled fully across his body Raven was in no doubt about Mac's need. She could feel his arousal pressing hotly against her. She moaned softly when his hand snaked down to slip beneath her T-shirt. Falling deeply into the kiss Raven ran her hands feverishly through his thick hair. Her body was plaster suggestively to his; when the gentle knock on the steamed window jarred her back to reality. "Mac!" she squeaked in a mortified whisper, before leaping back to the passenger seat.

"It's alright," he soothed helping her adjust her clothes. "The windows are steamed. No one can see anything."

"But they can surely guess what was going on," she cringed. She felt like crawling under the back seat. Inhaling deeply to steady her nerves, she released her breath slowly.

"Ready?" he asked. At her affirmative nod, he pressed the power window down slowly.

"Car trouble?" Brad joked peering into the dark interior.

"No," Mac responded brusquely. "What's going on?"

"I've been trying to reach you for hours," he commented. "Is your cell turned off?"

"I'm on a date," Mac responded as if that explained everything.

"Not anymore," Brad said with an apologetic shrug. "There's been another murder."

"Oh," Mac uttered suddenly alert.

"We need to check it out; hi Raven," Brad greeted when she turned towards him. "I thought that was you," he offered with a knowing smile.

"Hey Brad," she responded acutely embarrassed about being caught in the act, so to speak.

"I'll follow you," Mac barked not liking the way Brad was ogling Raven.

"Oh right," Brad said refocusing his attention on Mac.

{}

Mac pulled up to Baymiller Street for the second time in so many hours. Only this time, most of the broken down row houses were strewn across the road. Pulling up behind Brad's car, Mac could see they were examining the aftermath of an explosion. "Stay here," he directed at Raven before exiting his car. Following Brad towards the officer in charge of the crime scene he barked, "what'd we got?"

"They're bringing out a body now," he replied recognizing Mac as a senior detective. "It's badly burned, but dental records should give us a clear ID."

"The explosion?"

"Definitely not gas," he remarked reviewing his notes. "We'll start a thorough investigation once we get the all clear from the bomb squad. We did find this," he directed their attention to the duffle bag already tagged as evidence.

Slipping on a pair of latex gloves Mac began to meticulously sort through the contents of the bag. His face tightened into a hard mask when recognizing the product Luther had absconded with. He also spotted Luther's College ID and a CPD badge tucked in a side pocket. "I'll take this down to the station," he announced. Throwing all the items haphazardly back into the bag, he zipped the bag shut.

"You can't remove evidence from a crime scene," Brad cautioned when Mac headed towards his parked car.

"I can when the evidence in questions is going to be a shock to my girlfriend," he nodded towards his car. "It's best if she heard this from me."

"Falling in step beside him Brad asked, "you think it's wise to get involved with the sister of a murder…" was as far as he got when the evening air was suddenly pierced by Raven's hysterical scream. She'd grown tired of waiting for Mac and had clamored out of the car to see what was going on. Seeing Mac carrying Luther's bag as EMS carried a body to a nearby ambulance; she came to the only plausible conclusion.

"Take this," Mac said as he shoved the bag into Brad's surprised hands. "Raven," Mac murmured reaching her in two strides.

"Was that Luther?" she pointed shakily towards the ambulance.

"We don't know that yet."

"But that's his bag," she accused. "Why would his bag be here without him?" she demanded with rising hysteria.

Brad, standing a short distance away, was wondering the same thing. He would love to get Raven in an interrogation room for questioning. But Mac's dark look in his direction told him he would never get that chance. Watching him interact with Raven was an eye-opener. He was speaking to her in soft gentle tones. Whatever he was saying was having the desired effect. He was able to escort her calmly to his car, and settle her gently in the passenger seat.

Mac strode to where Brad was awkwardly holding Luther's bag to bark, "get me answers. I want to know the second they have a positive ID on the body."

"Sure thing," Brad replied. Clearing his throat, he voiced hesitantly, "but getting involved with a suspect's sister isn't the best…"

"I know what I'm doing," Mac scowled. "Just get me an ID."

Angling into his car, Mac pulled away from the curb. "Let me see it," Raven requested as they motored down the dark street.

"See what?" Mac asked surprised.

"What you put in your pocket. I saw you," she forestalled his interruption. "Before you tossed

Luther's bag to Brad, you slipped something in your pocket."

"You're mistaken."

"No," Raven said slowly. "I'm not."

"There's nothing in my pocket," he assured her. Giving her a brief glance, he said, "Brad is taking the bag and all of its contents to the station. Everything will be tagged as evidence. We don't know yet if this is tied in with your brother's case."

As lights from passing street lamps flickered across his face, Raven eyed him speculatively. He was lying. She had decided to trust him; yet within days of that trust, he was telling her a bold-faced lie. She had seen him remove evidence with her own eyes. But there he set trying to make it seem like she was crazy. "I know what I saw Mac," she uttered into the stilted silence.

Without another word, he reached inside his pocket and pulled out his badge, "happy now?" he queried at her stunned look.

"But you took this out of Luther's bag. How did it…"

"Obviously, someone's trying to set me up."

"Obviously," she murmured ill at ease. Mac

did it, she screamed silently in her head. He's the culprit. Mac killed my brother. I know that was Luther's body they dug out of the rubble. Oh lordy, lordy, lordy! I'm in the car with an axe murderer. He's murdered before I'm sure, she shuddered. Probably has several bodies buried in his basement. Criminee, she cringed feeling sick. I kissed a murdering psychopath. I have psychopath cooties.

"Aaaieeh!" she screamed when Mac placed his hand gently on her knee. Scooting to the far corner of the passenger seat she eyed his warily.

"You know my specialty is reading people," he voiced softly.

Cripes, she blanched aghast. He's reading me. He's going to kill me…he's going to kill me dead. They're going to find my bleached bones scattered across the mid-west. She had to get out, Raven realized. Looking frantically down the street, she decided that if the car slowed for an instant she was jumping out to make a run for it. Turning towards the door, she jiggled the handle. But Mac had it locked on his side. "Where are you taking me?" she asked with a definite quake in her voice.

"To your apartment," he replied. "Looks like you could use some chamomile tea." Giving her the once over he added, "and maybe some

Xanax." Speaking carefully, he said, "I gave that badge to Luther for his undercover work. Whoever nabbed him, obviously knows it belongs to me and is trying to draw me out."

"But who could've…"

"Everyone at the crime scene is a suspect. The only one I can reasonable rule out is you."

"Me!" Raven squeaked.

"You wear your heart and your emotions on your face. I was pretty much with you through every stage of your silent meltdown," he grinned. "If criminals were like you, my job would be a lot easier."

"Shut up," Raven intoned sheepishly.

"Like I said," he replied. "I'm trained to read people. Hardened criminals are a challenge to read. Civilians like you are a piece of cake."

"So…uh…what's our next move?" she asked, duly abashed about her freak out moment.

Grinning Mac chortled, "so you don't want to check out my basement for dead bodies?"

FOURTEEN

Picking up a clump of garlic from the shelf, Raven carried her bulb tray to an empty table. Long necked garlic with a mild sweet taste, she read. Autumn signaled the planting of garlic bulbs. She'd learned that much from her Master gardening courses.

"Don't mix the garlic," Hoover, the volunteer coordinator called out. "I want the long neck in one tray, extra spicy in another. Make sure you label your tray carefully before taking it to the misting area."

"Is he always this militant?" Mac whispered close to her ear.

Having arrived at the volunteer site without him, Raven was completely thrown to hear him so close to her ear. Jumping violently, she promptly dropped more than half of her soil onto the table. "Now look what you've made me do!" she hissed.

"Why didn't you wait for me?" he murmured.

"It's not always about what you want Mac," she answered vaguely.

Observing the raw tension marring her features, he asked, "what's that supposed to mean?"

Sighing heavily, she said, "I volunteer at the Arboretum once every three weeks. I merely realized today was my shift."

"With all that's going on you shouldn't keep the same routine," he advised. "Couldn't you put this volunteer stint off for the next few weeks?" At her noncommittal shrug, he said, "I don't want you leaving your apartment alone!" Lowering his voice because people around them were starting to stare avidly, he whispered, "it's not safe out there. Things are heating up fast with that explosion."

"Nature relaxes me," Raven informed him dully. "This relaxes me," she stressed as she cleared away the spilt soil.

"Is there a problem?" Hoover asked, appearing at the table.

"I need to talk to you," Mac voiced to the

coordinator before Raven could answer. Grabbing his arm, Mac steered him away from the table.

And good riddance to ya buddy, Raven silently scoffed at Mac's retreating back. Next time take a pill before you show up deluded and deranged. Just because he was keeping an eye on her, was no need for his paranoid behavior. Don't leave without me; wait for me; don't answer the phone, she silently mimicked his commands of late. With the body they'd hauled out of the rubble last night, she needed routine and normalcy in her life. Even a seasoned cop like Mac should appreciate that.

She'd just about finished her tray when Mac plunked down a bulb tray of his own. Snagging a chair with his leg he sat down. He then proceeded to shake his garlic packet in an exaggerated manner to insure all the bulbs fell to the bottom. Satisfied, he ripped the packet open and poured the bulbs in his big hand; all the while ignoring Raven as if she wasn't there.

When she couldn't stand his exaggerated show of enthusiasm any longer, she asked, "what are you doing?"

"Working on my bulb tray," he replied. He looked at her askance, as if she'd asked a stupid question.

"I can see that," Raven derided rolling her eyes. "I mean why do you have a bulb tray to begin with?"

"Oh that," he murmured poking a hole in a cell and dropping in a bulb. He covered the bulb with soil before saying, "I arranged with Hoover to acquire volunteer hours at the Arboretum."

"Why?" she asked completely bewildered by his behavior.

"Because you're here."

"But…"

"Get used to it!" he interrupted with a raw edge to his voice. "I told Luther I'd keep an eye on you, and I plan to do just that."

Gazing at him, it slowly dawned on Raven that her leaving the apartment had rattled him. "Were you worried that…"

"What do you think?" he grumbled not ready to be appeased.

"I'm sorry," she offered. "But all this cloak and dagger stuff is starting to mess with my brain. I needed to be around real people without all this sinister back drama."

"I thought you wanted more involvement in the case," he reminded her. "As I recall, and I'm quoting here ...sitting around waiting for news to trickle in will drive..."

"That was almost three weeks ago," Raven interrupted. "I thought the case would be over by now and everything would be back to normal. Now, a dead body was hauled out of a building."

"Juanita's death triggered the investigation," he pointed out.

"True," Raven conceded. "But I didn't see her body being lugged around." At his raised eyebrow of query, she said, "seeing a body taken from a broken building makes it too real. Plus, you were acting weird when you saw the body last night." Watching him shrewdly she noticed that even now he seemed uncomfortable.

"How was I acting?" he asked brusquely.

"Spooked...uh...no...surprised," she corrected. "You were acting like you weren't expecting to find a body there."

"It's always a surprise to stumble across a body. Even with my years of experience you never get comfortable with death."

Watching him carefully, Raven wondered if

he was telling her the truth; or feeding her a line. Aloud she said, "I'm starting to feel like a prisoner in my own apartment. I can't even take a leak without you hounding me with twenty questions. I can't hang out with friends, go to clubs or do anything I normally do. All I do is go to work and hang out with you," she finished accusingly.

"And that's a problem?"

Rolling her eyes at his lack of sensitivity, she replied, "a girl needs options Mac. What if I want to go out on a date?"

"Who with?" he asked aggressively.

"Who knows?" she shrugged. "My point is everyone thinks I'm dating you."

"Ah," he responded as comprehension dawned. "Carmelita has gotten word to your parents about our relationship?"

"We don't have a relationship."

"But they did call this morning, right?"

"What if they did," she responded irritated. "It's not like I can go see them without you tagging along. Nor can I tell them the true nature of our situation. I just wish this was over," she heaved.

"Luther got in trouble by knowing too much. I don't want that happening to you."

"Just tell me you're not involved in this, and that you're definitely one of the good guys," she appealed.

"I am one of the good guys," he murmured. The slight hesitation before he spoke had Raven staring at him intently. Was she being paranoid, she wondered; or maybe not paranoid enough.

"You hesitated just now," she mouthed. "Why?"

"Did I?" he muttered not meeting her eyes.

"You did," she stated emphatically.

Sighing, he reached for her hand. "You're going to have to trust that I'm doing all that I can to resolve all this."

"I know that," she agreed. "I just want your assurance that you're doing it legally; and not adding to the body count."

"I promise I'm not breaking any laws," he assured her.

"Good," she nodded. "And I should tell you things are starting to leak out. And my parents…well they're not stupid."

"What exactly did they say when they called this morning?"

"They're upset because they haven't been able to reach Luther in over a month. Naturally they blame me for not watching out for him in the big bad city."

"Where are your parents?"

"Nebraska."

"Where in Nebraska?"

"Lincoln, Nebraska. They are settling my grandparent's affairs. They passed away last year."

"Farmers?"

"Teachers, long retired," Raven corrected. "Lincoln is considered by many to be one of the jewels of the Mid-West. And no there is not a farmer or tractor salesman on every street corner."

"I stand corrected," Mac apologized.

"Anyway," Raven continued nodding her acceptance of his apology, "I had to tell them about Luther."

"And about me?"

"Yeah," she shrugged. "And without warning they went ballistic. Started ranting and raving that I should have been watching out for him; keeping him safe. They are determined to get to the bottom of this."

"Did you tell them I was FBI?"

"Of course not," she murmured. Feeling slighted that he'd think she'd break cover, she said, "and I didn't tell them Luther was working undercover when he disappeared."

"So why the sudden need to get out of the apartment?"

"I needed some air. They're threatening to come here and…"

"Who's threatening to come here?" Brad asked stopping at their table. Caught up in their conversation, neither had noticed him enter the room and quietly approach them.

About to answer truthfully, the warning squeeze on her knee from Mac had her saying, "my neighbor is threatening to drop off the cutest little kitten. He's a stray but they want to give him to a good home. I was just telling Mac that they're threatening to come here with kitten in hand."

"Um," Brad nodded staring at their clasped

hands on the table. "An odd choice of words for a pet. I thought maybe you were talking about a person."

"Nope," she murmured. She unconsciously held Mac's hand tighter at the raw aggression emanating from both men.

Are you two dating exclusively?" Brad asked an embarrassed Raven and smug Mac.

Her, "no of course not," and awkward attempt to disengage their hands was completely lost by Mac's bold assertion that they were.

"We're hanging out," Raven corrected glaring at Mac's adolescent aggression towards Brad.

"Because I would love to take you out to dinner sometime," Brad threw into their private glaring match."

"What?" Raven asked with eyes that widen briefly in surprise.

"Why are you here Brad?" Mac barked as if he was itching to start a fight with the man.

"The body," he said flicking out his notebook. "Coroner may have an ID. We're needed at the Station."

"This intel could have been provided by phone," Mac snarled abruptly. Irritated Brad was ogling Raven, he leaned forward and effectively shielded her with his big body.

"I was in the neighborhood," Brad smirked at Mac's shielding maneuver.

"Give me a minute to finish up here and I'll meet you at the Station," Mac spat with barely concealed rage. He did not like the way Brad was watching Raven.

"Sure thing," Brad offered with the same curiously intense look at Raven. He gave her a jaunty salute before heading for the door.

Watching him go Raven was thinking he moved with a grace and economy of movement one generally associated with athletes. "Are you quite finished with your lust fest?" Mac barked at the dreamily intent way she was watching Brad's retreating figure.

"I wasn't…" she began.

"If you were staring any harder, I'd have to arrest you for indecent behavior," he derided. Watching her face tighten in anger, he said, "I'll see you tonight."

"Tonight?"

"Have you forgotten I'm looking out for you?"

"No, I haven't," she said haughtily. "But I'm thinking that maybe you have. If I want to go out with Brad, I certainly can. To my knowledge, you and I are not a couple." Staring at her hotly, Mac swung on his heels and stormed from the Arboretum.

Now why had she said that, Raven wondered. Watching him stalk angrily away, she knew she was in trouble. Fighting her attraction to him by shifting into an argumentative shrew, was stupid; and with Mac's training, he would undoubtedly figure out the ruse. As handsome as Brad was, she was not attracted to him; and suspected he was not attracted to her. But for some reason, Brad was trying to rattle Mac's chain; catch him off guard. Perhaps like her, Brad was starting to suspect that Mac wasn't who he said he was; and the jury was still out on whether he could be trusted.

{}

Sitting crossed legged on Ash's hardwood floor, Raven leaned against the sofa as she nibbled on a slice of thin crusted pizza. She had long since kicked off her shoes, making herself right at home. After her stint at the Arboretum, she had met up with Ash for an afternoon at the salon. After a mani-pedi and massage, Raven had finally let go of the tension she'd carried since last night. They would have gone out for dinner, but seeing the cat lady lurking nearby, Raven decided against it. She did not want another public scene with her nemesis.

"What?" Ashley asked when Raven steered her in the opposite direction.

"You see the old crone trying to hide behind that pole?" she asked.

Following Raven's line of vision, she said, "yeah I see her."

"I gave her a dollar once. Now she's stalking me."

Grinning widely Ash said, "you're kidding."

"I wish I was. Seriously, I don't know how she keeps finding me," Raven heaved.

"She's harmless," Ash insisted. "Look at her?"

"The first time I met her she hit me. The second time she kept ramming her shopping cart into me."

Giggling unrepentantly Ash said, "but you have fighting skills that are combat ready. Surely you could take her out easily enough."

"And make the news for beating down a homeless old lady?"

"Well, what are we going to do for dinner then? I'm starving. I have to eat something."

Purchasing two pizzas they made their way to Ash's apartment. She and Ash had now moved on to stuffing their faces; while trying to solve a murder, with very little factual data to go on. It had been Ashley's idea to construct a murder board like they do on TV; that way, they could develop a time line and determine where everyone was. Gazing at the murder board thoughtfully, Raven asked, "what do we really know about Juanita? It all started with her."

"And Luther," Ash reminded. "Don't forget Luther."

"Exactly, now were they dating or merely undercover?"

"Could be a lover's triangle that ended badly," Ash offered.

"Mummmm," Raven agreed taking a drink from her soda. "Gary is also a big part of this equation."

"The pharmacy student?" Ash queried.

"Not any more. He's been AWOL from class for a while now. No one seems to know where he is or what he's up to."

"But I thought he and Luther were pretty tight. At the family barbeque, last June, they spent all that time…"

"I know," Raven coughed trying to cover her snicker. Ash had been pretty miffed that Luther wasn't noticing her; choosing instead to converse with Gary most of the time. They claimed they were trying to work the bugs out of their latest lab project.

"Lab project my eye," Ash hmphed. "I bet they were…"

"What's all this?" Mac rumbled from the doorway.

"It's alright Ash," Raven quickly inserted. Noting Ash was looking terrified that a strange man was in her apartment, she added, "this is Mac, my jailer."

"Mac," Ash murmured worriedly. "How did you get into my apartment?"

"I want to say the door was open," he began contritely. "But the truth is I broke in; haven't met a lock yet that I couldn't crack."

"But why did…"

"I was concerned about Raven."

"You thought she was in danger?"

"Not really," he supplied sheepishly. "I could hear the two of you giggling in the hall. I figured if I knocked, she would convince you not to let me in."

"Oh," Ash murmured looking from Raven to Mac.

Taking in the nearly empty pizza box on the table he asked hopefully, "is there anymore pizza?" When Ash went to retrieve the second pizza from the kitchen he asked Raven, "are you still mad at me?" Taking a seat, he gazed at her hungrily. She was wearing blue jeans rolled up at the ankles and her cream cropped sweater. She looked relaxed and very sexy.

"I wasn't mad at you," Raven shrugged. "But your world is driving me batty; and being on lockdown certainly doesn't help."

"I'm trying to keep you safe. Being out of

the limelight is the best way I know how to do that."

"I know," Raven voiced softly. She would have said more, but Ash chose that moment to plunk the second pizza on the coffee table.

"So, Mac," she crooned. "What are your intentions with Raven?" Sitting on the arm of his chair, she waited for his answer expectantly.

"Honorable," Mac grinned. "Definitely honorable."

"They'd better be," she announced suddenly aggressive. "Cause I don't care what kind of special Seal training you have. You hurt her and I'll…"

"Cut it out Ash!" Raven blared.

"I'm just saying," she replied. Looking Mac up and down, she narrowed her eyes on him suspiciously.

"Really Ash," Raven voiced sarcastically. With a rueful shake of her head, she said, "I seem to recall someone hearing a noise inside of an apartment and running away like a little girl with pigtails."

Moving towards the kitchen to grab Mac a beer, Ash pointed her fingers at her eyes and then at

Mac; signaling she would be watching him.

"Wow," he replied with a boyish grin. "So that's tall girl?"

"Yes."

"She's scary."

"She's tall but a feather weight. I'm sure you could snap her like a twig."

"Possibly," he replied. "But it's the scrawny ones you have to watch out for."

Smiling, she looked at Mac with affection. With his windswept hair, oversized sweat shirt and jeans he looked adorable. It would be nice if he was a real person. Someone over for just a casual evening, she mused.

"I am a real person," he voiced.

"You know what I mean; and I thought we agreed you weren't going to use your super powers on me."

"Come again?" he asked.

"Stop reading me. If I don't voice it out loud you aren't allowed to comment on my thoughts."

"You're so easy to read," he purred.

"Hmph," she mouthed. "You're not a difficult read either. I just exercise tact and decorum by allowing you privacy with your inner thoughts."

"Really?" he queried.

"Yes really," she beamed smugly

"Ok then, what am I thinking now?"

Eyeing him shrewdly, she snorted, "pervert. You're thinking about sex."

"With you in the room, that's always on my mind."

"Uh, do they have a positive ID on the body they found last night?"

Smiling broadly at her blatant segue in changing the subject, he said, "not yet."

"But I thought Brad said they had an ID. Wasn't that why he was at the Arboretum this morning?"

"No," Mac replied. "He was there hoping to get you alone. Finding me there forced him to improvise."

"Why does he want me alone?"

"He wants to sweat you for information about Luther." When her eyes widened in alarm, he said, "don't worry. That is never gonna happen on my watch."

Brad was turning into a real pain, Mac decided. He knew Brad was keeping tabs on him; watching his every move; waiting for him to slip up. He would have to speed up his timeline if he wanted to stay a step ahead of Brad.

Munching quietly on pizza, Mac took in her murder board. He noticed she had separated the evidence into four columns. In three of them he was the prime suspect; while the cat lady was the prime suspect in the fourth column. "Am I a suspect?" he chuckled.

Placing a beer on the table beside him, Ash answered, "you are the common denominator between Luther, Gary and Juanita."

"Why is Sadie a suspect?" he wondered.

"She's a person of interest," Raven said.

"Because of the beat down outside the station?" he asked innocently.

"Don't start," she intoned. "And for the last

time, I tripped."

"If you say so," he smiled like the proverbial Cheshire cat. Looking closely in Juanita's column he snickered, "I was dating Juanita?"

"And Gary," Ash pointed out. "And Sadie the cat lady," she chuckled.

"She's sixty-five," he voiced scandalized.

"What can I say," Ash shrugged. "You like 'em old."

"Really," he appealed to Raven.

"Hey," she chortled, "not my idea. We're just tossing out theories here."

"May I make a suggestion?"

"Sure thing," Ash replied. Picking up the marker, she stood primed to write his suggestion on the board.

"Leave police work to policemen," he advised. "No more murder boards and no more visiting victim's apartments."

"You're one to talk," Ash derided. "You took Raven on a stakeout."

"Only to show her how dangerous

investigating can be; especially when you don't know what you're doing or what you're getting yourself into. Things can change in an instant and you have to be ready."

"Which she was," Ash reminded.

"Yes," Mac agreed watching Raven tenderly. "She was."

FIFTEEN

Things were getting dicey, Mac admitted, as he entered the Station two days later. Brad's meddlesome poking was going to have to be dealt with. Raven was becoming more guarded around him; and Stella was nearly at her breaking point. The explosion on Baymiller seemed to have spooked them both. Raven, because she thought her brother was found in the rubble; and Stella, because she knew her associates were getting twitchy. When people got twitchy in Stella's world, they tended to tie up loose ends quickly; and by his estimate, Stella was definitely a loose end. "Reid!" he barked into his cell phone.

"That explosion on Baymiller…" Stella began near hysterics.

"We've been over this Stella."

"You don't understand!" she interrupted on a frightened gasp. "I was in that building minutes before it blew. I think it was meant for me."

"Keep it together," he demanded at the quake in her voice. As the elevator inched its way to the second floor, he said, "Brad and I are looking into the explosion."

"But Mac," she began.

"Later," he replied brusquely ending the call.

Stella was starting to lose it. He'd stop by the museum later and deal with her; time to let her know who was running this operation. Exiting the lift, he found Brad waiting for him. "You're not going to believe this," he voiced surprised.

"The body found in the rubble wasn't Luther," Mac guessed as he fell in step beside him.

"Got it in one," Brad uttered. "It was a Gary Randall. He was a person of interest in the..." Caught up in his detailed analysis, Brad didn't notice Mac's smug smile before he quickly masked it by lowering his head to check his watch.

"Uh, so who's in the morgue?" Mac asked trying to sound surprised.

"Gary Randall," Brad repeated. "We're still trying to piece together his movements leading up to the explosion."

"Could he have been a squatter?" Mac asked.

"We'll look into that angle, but he did have a place near campus. CSU is going over his place now. Evidence indicates he was there as recently as a week ago."

"Um," Mac observed. Shifting through files on his desk, he looked up inquiringly when Brad cleared his throat.

"Er, you don't think this could be related to the Jahoda case?" Brad asked.

"How so?"

"I only suggest it because Gary was Luther's lab partner." Watching Mac's reactions closely, he said, "Gary is dead and Luther's bag was found in the rubble with a fair amount of drugs. Obviously, Luther was in the building on Baymiller at some point."

"Or maybe Gary took the bag to the building. You said yourself they were lab partners. It would have been easy for Gary to shift blame from himself to Luther by planting that bag."

"Maybe," Brad remarked not convinced. "I think we need to bring in the sister and sweat…" Mac's look of murderous fury had him holding up both hands in a conciliatory manner and saying, "but I'll let you handle questioning the sister."

Leafing through the file on Gary, Mac barked, "anything else?"

"Just that we have surveillance footage of Baymiller Street prior to the explosion." A woman hovering on the street has been identified as Stella Mann. She was seen leaving the building just before it blew."

"Prostitute?" Mac suggested.

"Not likely," Brad supplied. "But the timing is too coincidental to discount. She may have seen something or set the explosion herself," he argued.

"Do we have a home address?"

"This chick is definitely hiding something," Brad replied. "Her home address is sketchy. We looked up her driver's license. The address listed is an abandoned building in Lawndale. But her work address is the Field Museum."

Taking the slip of paper from Brad's outstretched hand, Mac said, "I'll talk to her." Before leaving he turned to Brad and asked, "the night of the explosion, how did you find me on my date?"

"I tracked your cell phone."

"Why?"

"We're partners. We are supposed to be working this case together and ciphering through clues together. You're holding out on me man. You won't let me anywhere near Raven who could…"

"She is not involved in any way." Mac interrupted harshly. Turning abruptly, he strode from the office.

"Interesting," Brad whispered at his angry exit.

{}

Bounding up the steps to the museum, Raven was more than happy to be rid of Mac's company, if only for a little while. He had been in a cuddly mood all weekend. But Raven had felt guarded; not sure if she could trust him. She was in a strange place where her heart said go for it; but her intellect said no frigging way. And she certainly did not want to repeat the mistakes of Derek, she shuddered. Mac had told her next to nothing about the body found in the rubble. He had been equally silent on Luther's duffle bag found at the crime scene. If Mac wanted her to trust him, then he had better start giving her some straight answers. Real answers, she fumed as she entered the museum. Her grim look was immediately replaced by mild concern when she encountered a highly-agitated Stella.

Stella was not looking her best. She was jittery, as if she'd thrown herself together in a hurry. What was worse, was the look of real fear on her face.

"What's wrong Stella?" Raven asked.

"I need to talk to you," she began. "It's about Juanita and Mac."

"What about them?"

"Mac isn't…" looking past Raven, Stella's eyes widened with unmitigated fear. Surprised, Raven turned to find Brad entering the building.

"If you're looking for Mac, he's not here," Raven informed him.

"Actually, I was looking for you," he smiled politely.

"Mac already told me you're trying to sweat me for information about Luther; which I don't have."

"Aw, I'm hurt," he uttered clutching his chest. "And here I thought we were friends. Did I or did I not rescue you from the cat lady?"

"Don't go there," she grinned.

"You owe me," he charmed with a dimpled smile.

"Mac really isn't here, so I don't know what I can help you with."

"I know Mac isn't here," he confessed. "I was tailing him when he stopped off at his apartment."

"Why were you tailing him," Raven frowned.

"He was coming to question Stella." Stella jerked violently when hearing Mac wanted to question her. Her reaction caused Brad and Raven to stare at her with concern.

"What's wrong Stella," Raven asked.

"Yeah Stella," Brad uttered. "What were you saying about Mac and Juanita?"

"N nothing," she stuttered stumbling awkwardly back.

"Perhaps you and I need to have a conversation downtown Stella."

"Do you have an arrest warrant Brad?" Raven asked.

"I see Mac's teaching you about police protocol," he casually remarked.

"Among other things," Raven insinuated.

Gazing at Raven with a look of admiration that she was calling his bluff, he turned to Stella with, "don't leave town." Favoring Raven with another of his jaunty salutes, he turned and left the museum.

"Stella!" Charles chirped as he entered the building. "How was your weekend girlfriend?"

"Ugh," Stella moped before turning and disappearing into the museum crowd.

"What'd I say?" Charles worried.

Normally he and Stella not only greeted each other in Ebonics; but also, engaged in an elaborate hand shake ritual that made Charles feel as if he was assimilating into the African American culture. "I'm sure it's nothing," Raven tried to soothe. "I think she's in a hurry to set up for the staff meeting. Uh, it starts in five minutes. I'll see you later Charles."

{}

At the Field Museum, Mac strolled over to a nearby tour group. He had changed into jeans and a popular basketball hoodie. The getup made him look like a run of the mill guy; rather than a seasoned FBI agent. Blending discreetly with the crowd, he kept an eagle eye out for Stella. He needed to neutralize her before she slipped and got them both killed. As the tour group ambled along, Mac spotted Stella as she exited the elevator. She was in a state, he saw. Agitated and downright scared. She undoubtedly knew what was coming. Slipping unobtrusively from the tour, he followed her stealthy to the stock room. About to pounce, he dived quickly behind a pillar when he saw she was meeting Raven.

"There you are," Raven began hearing Stella approach. Kneeling beside an open crate, she was rummaging through it carefully. "You left the staff meeting early so I didn't get the chance to tell you…" Hearing Stella whimper Raven looked up surprised. "Good lord Stella, what happened to you?" she asked.

"I need your help," she uttered worriedly. Raven was shocked to see Stella had been crying. Her disheveled appearance was equally surprising. Stella was normally polished and well manicured.

"Okay," Raven replied. Rising slowly to her feet, she waited for Stella to continue. At eye level, she could see Stella was shaking. Something had spooked her badly and she wrung her hands as her eyes darted fearfully around the stock room.

"No one was supposed to get hurt," she blurted.

"Okay," Raven encouraged when she fell silent again.

"It all started about nine months ago. We thought we could make some quick cash by hiding…"

"Aaaah!" she yelped when Mac stepped around the pillar.

Turning to see what had frightened her this time, Raven frowned. "What are you doing here Mac?"

"I'm taking Stella into police custody," he answered lazily."

"No," Stella moaned backing away. "Raven he's…"

"That's enough," Mac warned. "Anything you say can and will be used against you." With his eyes narrowed on her purposely, he grasped her upper arm in a vice like hold.

Stella was terrified, Raven saw. Tears gathered in her eyes began to fall unheeded down her face. "What's this about Mac?"

"Police business," he answered curtly. "I do have an arrest warrant," he assured her.

"Raven," Stella pleaded on a barely audible whisper as Mac marched her out of the stockroom.

"Stella, do you want me to come with you?" Raven voiced in response to her barely audible plea. With a frightened look at Mac, Stella nodded yes.

But Mac forestalled her joining them by stating bluntly, "this is a police investigation. Stella is under arrest. You can meet her at the station once she's processed."

Stunned at Mac's abrupt behavior, Raven felt like kicking him. He offered a curt nod to

Charles when he strode into the stockroom. He then proceeded to practically drag the whimpering Stella out. Charles gasp of surprise was completely ignored by Mac; and went unnoticed by Stella.

"What was that about?" Charles asked a bemused Raven.

"Stella's been arrested," she absently replied.

"What for?"

"I'm not sure," she shrugged. "Stella was about to tell me when Mac swooped in and arrested her."

SIXTEEN

Raven arrived at the Station with a very neurotic Charles in tow. He had insisted on accompanying her, claiming Stella needed him. Since Stella barely registered his existence on a good day; Raven thought that was highly unlikely. But he had insisted and she had given in to his pathetic wheedling. The thirty minute drive to the Station had felt more like five hours; because his nervous and fidgety behavior was driving her nuts. He had harped on Stella's predicament the entire way over; going through every worst case scenario he could think of. The man would not shut up, Raven silently heaved as she angled out of the car.

"You know Stella is a delicate flower," he expounded in his twittery voice. "She's not like us," he continued as he stumbled out of the car. "She's not made for prison."

"And I am?" Raven demanded, stopping dead in her tracks.

"You know what I mean," he dismissed with an agitated flick of his hand. "We have to help Stella." Racing up the steps, he looked back somewhat irritated at her sedate pace. "Come on!" he chirped holding the door. "We have to help Stella." Poor sap, Raven thought as he waited impatiently for her to catch up; she doesn't even know you exist. Fed up with Raven moving with the viscosity of thick molasses, Charles dashed inside.

When Raven entered the building, she saw Charles arguing with the desk sergeant.

"She has to be here," he beseeched. "Your detective brought her in."

"Sorry," the desk sergeant calmly replied. Viewing Charles as a minor irritant, he searched his records again before stating emphatically, "we have no record of a Stella Mann being arrested or brought in for questioning today."

Thunderstruck Charles turned to Raven, "she's not here," he bleated.

"That can't be right. Mac said he was bringing her in. She must be in processing or something."

Turning to the desk sergeant hopefully, Charles was met with disappointment when he said, "there is no record of a Stella Mann in processing."

"Is detective Mac Reid in?" Raven asked.

"Not at the moment."

"Uh, what about his partner, Brad Hobart?"

"I'll ring his desk. Have a seat."

Making their way to the bench under the window, Raven groaned inwardly. Sadie, the cat lady was sneaking stealthy from a nearby bathroom. Oh joy, Raven cringed; my stalker. Turning towards Charles, she hoped the old crone wouldn't notice her. But for someone who wore an eye patch, she had an eagle eye. Spotting Raven, she made a beeline in her direction.

"You reporting me?" she demanded somewhat aggressively.

"No," Raven intoned woodenly. Seriously, she silently griped, how does she keep finding me?

"Your man?" she jerked in Charles' direction.

"Co-worker," Raven hastily replied. Sadie

was watching Charles so intently; Raven feared she might clonk him on the head if she didn't vouch for him. Feeling the pressure of the cat lady's intense stare down, Charles squirmed uncomfortably. Raven was spared the awkwardness of trying to reel in the cat lady's rude behavior when she suddenly took off. Looking to see what had spooked her, she saw Brad rapidly approaching.

"Was that…" he began with a huge grin.

"It was," Raven interrupted. She could tell by his lopsided smile that he was recalling their earlier encounter.

She felt her own lips twitching into a grin when Charles blurted, "where is Stella? I'm here to pay her bail."

Charles was back to speaking in his fast, tremulous manner; so, Brad looked to Raven enquiringly. "Mac was at the museum earlier. He arrested Stella and brought her in for questioning," she interpreted.

"Sorry, they haven't arrived yet."

"But that was more than two hours ago," Charles whined.

Frowning his concern, Brad wondered what Mac was playing at. He was going completely off the rails lately. Disappearing for hours at a time, arresting suspects without him; now he was in the wind with a legitimate person of interest. "I'm sure he'll be here shortly," Brad soothed.

"What kind of rinky-dink outfit is this?" Charles demanded. "She was taken from work. That can't be legal," he sputtered aggressively. "Kidnapping a private citizen can't be…"

"Nothing to worry about," Brad inserted. "They should be arriving any minute."

But even to Raven's ears, he sounded doubtful. She shrugged noncommittally when Charles looked to her for clarification.

"I knew this would happen," he whined. Revisiting his worst case scenario theories, he bleated, "he could have her tied to a chair by now," he predicted.

"Don't be ridiculous," Raven voiced a little embarrassed at his outburst. Rolling her eyes that his worst case scenarios were getting weirder by the second she asked, "why would Mac tie Stella to a chair?"

"Sex!" Charles adamantly brayed. "Everybody want's Stella."

"No, you want Stella," Mac corrected lazily.

Taken aback by his sudden appearance, they all watched him stroll casually into the Station without Stella.

"Where's Stella?" Charles asked belligerently.

"She got away," Mac shrugged nonchalantly.

"From you!" they all chorused in disbelief.

"It happens," he replied sheepishly. "Stella was desperate and didn't want to go back to prison."

"Back?" Raven queried.

"I ran her prints. They came up as a Teri King; wanted for insurance and credit card fraud in Seattle."

"This is precisely why I should be in on the take down," Brad admonished. "She would not have gotten away from both of us."

"Sorry," Mac admitted. "But I thought I could bring her in. I wasn't counting on how desperate she was."

"Where is she now?" Charles asked in a hopeless whisper.

"More than halfway to Canada is my guess.

I put out an APB on her so the entire country will be on the lookout."

Looking like he was sucking a sour lemon, Charles gasped, "did you hurt her, is she okay?"

"More than okay," Mac chuckled ruefully. "The girl has to be something of a contortionist to escape handcuffs and a locked car."

"It's not funny!" Charles yelled when Brad joined in the laughter. "Stella is a delicate flower! She doesn't understand the streets!"

"Uh, I think they're laughing that a big guy like Mac was outwitted by a petite girl," Raven murmured into the awkward silence his outburst had caused. "I think I should get Charles home," she added.

Mac stopped her from leaving by saying, "actually Raven I need to talk to you about Stella and any known associates."

"We just work together. I really don't know anything about her private life."

"Brad do you mind getting Charles home?" Not waiting for an answer, he led Raven briskly down the hall to his office.

"Okay, where's Stella?" Raven whispered

the second they were out of earshot.

"Witness protection," Mac voiced quietly.

"Did she talk?"

"Sang like a canary. I know everything now."

"Is it over now?"

"Not quite. There are a few lose ends to tie up, and then we can get down to the business of a relationship."

"Oh really?" Raven grinned.

"Yes really," he grinned right back.

{}

Snuggling close to Mac, Raven sighed with contentment. After a wonderfully romantic dinner, they now set in his hearth room listening to a crackling fire; while gazing lazily at the scenic beauty of Lincoln Park. The multi-colored leaves were beautiful. The windswept trees insured the park grounds were bathed in a thick carpet of dazzling color. The sun setting over the entire scene was breathtaking. It felt like they were in the middle of an enchanted forest. If a hobbit popped out of a tree, she wouldn't be surprised Raven grinned.

"What's so funny," Mac murmured hugging her close.

"I thought I saw a hobbit," she answered. She felt him smile as he gently nuzzled her neck. "Mac," she groaned when he released the clasp on her bra.

"Hmmm," he uttered as he palmed her breast.

"We are not having sex," she stated emphatically.

"We're making love."

"We're not doing that either," she replied. Reaching behind, she clasped her bra.

"Why not?"

"It's too fast." At his, I object expression she said, "I want this whole thing with Luther cleared up and a chance to get to know you as a real person," she preempted his next objection.

"We could just fool around," he encouraged.

"No, we can't because it'll only lead to one thing and you know it."

"I have the fortitude of a Monk," he boasted. "I won't let things go too far."

"I'm not wired that way. I don't want to get all riled up just to douse myself with ice water. "

"You want me bad," he purred.

"Shut up," she grinned tossing a pillow at him.

He avoided it easily before replying, "the feeling is mutual. I want you just as bad," he uttered hoarsely. Giving her a deeply passionate kiss on the lips he griped, "now try not to attack me while I find something distracting for us to watch on TV."

"Funny," she teased. As he absently flicked through channels Raven laughed, "uh, Mac?"

"What?" he asked innocently.

"Your hand," she pointed out.

Looking down he saw his hand was under her shirt inching towards her bra clasp again. "How'd that get there?" he wondered. Snatching his hand away he uttered, "this thing has a mind of its own."

Raven was laughing happily when Stella's picture appeared on the screen. Leaning forward she grabbed Mac's hand. "Wait, Mac go back," she voiced urgently. "That was Stella on the screen."

Switching back two channels they heard the reporter announce...

The body found along the shore of Lake Michigan has been positively identified as Stella Mann. She was a known....

Mac switched off the TV when Raven turned to him with horrified eyes. "I thought you said she was in witness protection."

"She was," he tried to soothe.

But when he reached for her she leapt back and yelped, "stay away from me!"

"There's a leak on the force which is why the FBI was brought in, remember?" He spoke soothingly and slowly; as if he was trying to calm a skittish horse.

"You were the last person to see her alive," she accused.

"No, her killer was the last one to see her

alive," he corrected. "I have been with you all day."

Watching him shrewdly, Raven didn't know what to think. Mac had disappeared for two hours; allegedly to put Stella in protective custody. He'd had plenty of time to kill her and dispose of the body. Plus, he had that cockamamie story that Stella had over powered him and gotten away. Stella was only a little taller than she was, Raven reasoned. There was just no way she could have over powered Mac and made a run for the border.

"I never said she over powered me," he quietly inserted.

Raven flinched violently when realizing Mac was reading her again. Trying to make her mind go blank, she reached for her purse and began to edge awkwardly towards the door.

"Raven, let me explain," he began. When he started to stalk her steps, she gave up all pretense of leaving with dignity. She turned and ran screaming from the room. She raced through the kitchen and slammed out of the house. Once she was locked safely in her car, she breathed a sigh of relief. Looking up, she saw Mac was standing on his back deck. There was an alert stillness about him. No doubt he was plotting how best to kill her and dispose of the remains, she frowned. His whole persona was starting to scream psychotic killer, she shuddered. As she pulled out of his drive, Raven was more than half convinced Mac was a killer. What she couldn't figure out was why said killer had let her get away.

SEVENTEEN

"Are you sure?" Ash asked as she watched Raven pace frantically back and forth in her living room. Raven had arrived on her doorstep an hour ago, with an outrageous story about Mac. Ash had only met Mac once; but from what she could tell, he seemed like a pretty standup guy.

"Sure, I'm sure," Raven said with conviction. "Stella's death was on the news. They found her body on the shore of…"

"You don't have a TV," Ash casually reminded.

"I was at Mac's house when the story broke."

"What were you doing there?"

"Having dinner, watching the sun set, relaxing on the sofa. What does it matter?" she flailed. "The point is Mac…"

"How relaxed?" Ashley interrupted with a girlish squeal.

"We weren't having sex if that's what you're getting at," Raven scowled. "I just had a life altering experience and all you can think about is sex?"

"So far, I don't see anything life altering about tonight," she shrugged. "I mean did Mac attack you?"

"Well no but…"

"Did he act in a menacing or threatening manner?"

"No, but psychopaths are known to reel you in with their unassuming demeanor. Remember that Dahmer crack pot? He worked in a candy factory."

"Uh huh," Ash replied unconvinced. "Exactly, what did Mac do that spooked you so badly? I mean he didn't attack you. He wasn't threatening or anything, was he?"

"He walked towards me in a very psychotic manner," Raven offered.

"Which means?"

"It was slow and creepy, like he was going to hang my entrails from his clothes line; or toss my toes in a vat of chili."

"Human chili, ugh," Ash shuddered. Chortling softly, she tried to look repentant at Raven's dark frown. "I'm sorry Raven," she soothed. "But I'm just not getting psychotic killer from any of this."

"But Stella's body was found dead on the beach. Mac arrested her and disappeared for two hours. He was the last one to see her alive."

"No, her killer, whoever that is; was the last one to see her alive."

"What are you, his public relations manager now?" Raven asked sarcastically.

"I'm just saying anyone could have gotten to Stella. You said yourself she was into some pretty shady stuff."

"Only a cop could have gotten to Stella," Raven derided. "She was in protective custody, remember?"

"True, but who knew she was in protective custody besides Mac?"

"No one," Raven began slowly. "Unless he told his partner and I don't think he would have done that."

"And why not, they're partners," Ash argued.

Considering Mac was most likely a deranged killer; Raven decided all bets about his supposedly undercover work were off. Besides that, she reasoned, she would trust Ash with her life. And if she ended up in his bone collection, Ash would be able to direct the authorities right to his door. "Mac's undercover," she blurted as she sat beside Ash on the sofa. At her quizzical look, she said, "no one at the Station is supposed to know he's working undercover."

Tossing back her head, Ash laughed outright. "That makes no sense," she grinned. "Someone at that Station has to know. Someone had to arrange his presence there and someone has to be providing backup."

"Unless of course Mac is a dirty cop; and this whole, I'm FBI, is just a poly to lull me into a false sense of security," Raven argued.

"He doesn't strike me as a cop on the take."

"That's because you didn't see the look in

his eyes when I pulled out of his drive," Raven replied.

"Which was?"

"There was a quiet stillness about him. Like he was plotting how best to do me in and dispose of the remains."

"Maybe he was wondering what seasonings would go best with an archeologist," she snickered. But seeing real worry in Raven's eye's, she voiced bluntly, "you're over reacting. Just like the time you thought you saw old man Fuller and his wife shimmy down the flag pole."

"That was different."

"Or the time you thought your elderly neighbor was involved in old lady porn; or the time you were convinced a local ENT physician was panhandling on Michigan Avenue or the time…"

Twisting her lips in a wry grimace Raven admitted, "it's been a tense eight weeks. Maybe I did overact a little."

"You ran from his house screaming," Ash reminded on an irreverent chuckle. "And you had the nerve to make fun of me for running from Juanita's brownstone."

"I'm an idiot," Raven heaved dropping her head in her hands. "Mac must think I'm a total basket case."

"I think he was mostly worried." Raising her head, Raven stared at Ashley surprised. "Ok he might have called and told me you were upset and on your way over."

"But how did he know where to find me?"

"He followed you the entire way."

"Criminy, he must think I'm a total nut job."

"He does. He said your driving was erratic; that you were weaving in and out of traffic like a maniac."

"He called me a maniac?" Raven asked highly offended.

"He called your driving erratic and maniacal, but I think he likes you anyway," Ash grinned.

"Ugh, how am I going to face him again?"

"We'll talk about that tomorrow. Tonight, it's wine, chocolate and romantic comedies. We'll tackle the Mac issue after a good night's sleep."

"I don't want to go home tonight," Raven

uttered worriedly.

"Which is why the guest room is made up and ready to go. Mac thought it best if you bunked here tonight," she explained at Raven's surprised look. "He figured the way you were maneuvering in and out of traffic like a clumsy James Bond; you wouldn't want to face Chicago's traffic scene again tonight."

"Shut up," Raven said at her amused chuckle.

{}

Yawning her way to Ash's kitchen, Raven stopped abruptly when she encountered Mac. He was sitting casually at the breakfast table as if he didn't have a care in the world. "What are you doing here?" she asked surprised.

"Waiting for you." Watching her carefully, he thought she looked adorable wearing shorts and a tee shirt. The clothes clearly belonged to Ashley, he thought; because her girls were practically straining at the seams to get out. Feeling his body heating, he stood and pulled out a seat. "May I?" he offered.

"Thank you," Raven voiced quietly. She

was feeling keenly embarrassed about her hysterical melt down. She'd practically accused him of being a deranged murderer. She had run from his house as if the hounds of hell were on her heels. "Uh, where's Ashley?" she asked awkwardly.

"She let me in and went to work; after I fed her," he grinned. "That girl is part rhino. You're lucky there's anything left for you."

"Um," Raven nodded. Taking in the large spread on the table, she was amazed there was so much left. Ashley really did have a healthy appetite for one so thin.

"She said you had a key so you could lock up the place," he replied to her nod. "Toast?" he offered in the awkward silence.

"Thanks," she murmured. Taking a cautious sip of orange juice, she twisted her lips wryly. She didn't know what to say or how to respond to Mac.

"The juice isn't poisoned. You can gulp it down if you want," he said. His wicked grin prompted a similar grin in her.

"I'm sorry," she mouthed. "I don't know what I was thinking."

"I heard you thought I was a cannibal after your entrails for my clothes line and your best bits for my chili."

In the harsh light of day, her ranting seemed extremely ridiculous and she had to choke back a giggle. "Okay, I was over the top," she admitted.

"And now?" he asked.

"I'm an idiot," she shrugged. "I also realize I'm not cut out for this cloak and dagger stuff. I'm getting paranoid, seeing monsters everywhere."

"Good to have you back in the world of the sane," he admitted.

"If it's any consolation no one's safe," she assured him. "Yesterday when Brad stopped by the museum, I practically accused him of being a dirty cop,'" she said with a rueful shake of her head.

"Brad was at the museum?" Mac asked suddenly alert.

"He claimed he was there to talk to Stella and I sort of demanded he show me an arrest warrant."

"When was this?"

"Yesterday morning. But he didn't take her," Raven said.

"Did you tell him Stella was in witness

protection?"

"No. I was…"

"Were you alone with him at any time?"

"He pulled me aside at the Station yesterday. We talked briefly about my cat lady problem. But Charles was right there and we were never out of eyesight of the desk sergeant." She answered. Concerned Mac was watching her with a sense of urgency she asked, "what's wrong?"

"Where's your purse?" he asked rising from the table. Following him, Raven retrieved her purse from the guest room. Handing the purse to Mac; she watched as he dumped the contents on the coffee table. He then proceeded to meticulously cipher through every item, every scrap of paper and every pen. He finally found what he was looking for when he picked up a tiny silk leafed pin. Placing his finger to his lips, he signaled her not to speak. Raven hovered on his heels as he approached the breakfast table and dropped the pin in a glass of water.

"What was that?" she asked.

"You were wired," he uttered grimly.

"Did Brad plant that on me?"

"This is policeman issue," he said. Holding up the glass, he examined the water-logged contraption closely. "Only someone in law enforcement would have access to this kind of tech."

"What does this mean?"

"It means he heard me tell you Stella was in witness protection. Only a cop could have gotten to her."

Raven was feeling sick. She felt the pit of her stomach drop to the vicinity of her knees. Taking a seat before she keeled over, she murmured, "I thought you said this was nearly over."

"With Stella's testimony, it was. Now it seems we are back to square one."

When he squirmed uncomfortably she asked, "what else does it mean Mac?"

"It means Brad may see you as bait and is itching to tie up loose ends."

"He seemed so nice," Raven voiced worriedly.

"Brad knew I was planning to stop by the museum to talk to Stella. My guess is he scurried to

246

get there and ran into you."

"Me!" Raven asked surprised. "Why would that stop him?"

"If he had taken Stella, you would have been able to testify that he was the last one to see her alive. Remember I told you Luther got close to the target. He disappeared before he could tell us who that was." Swallowing fearfully, Raven listened stunned. "I think Brad is tailing you. Hoping you will lead him to Luther. That's why he showed up at the Arboretum and that's why he put a trace on you."

"Do you think Luther is still alive?"

"He has to be," Mac assured her. At her doubtful look, he said, "otherwise Brad would not have felt the need to bug you. Clearly he's hoping you can lead him to Luther."

"And if that happens?"

"He'll kill you both and get out clean."

"I can't believe this is happening," she shuddered. Her stomach was in knots and she felt like she was going to upchuck everything in her stomach from the past forty-eight hours. "Did he kill Juanita?"

"I'm not sure," Mac said. "But he may have planted the bomb on Baymiller."

"Why," Raven croaked.

"He's tying up loose ends. Gary's dead. He was found in the explosion on Baymiller." When she flinched violently at hearing the news of Gary's death, Mac continued grimly, "Brad drew attention to Stella by producing surveillance footage of her loitering on Baymiller."

"Why is that suspicious?"

"There are no surveillance cameras on Baymiller; so the footage is definitely fabricated. I'm guessing he's also the one who planted my badge at the scene."

"But you found the badge so you're in the clear, right?"

"No. It means Brad knows who I am; or has a pretty good idea. He may have been trying to send me the message that he is on to me."

"What do we do now?" she asked on a nervous whisper.

"Can you take the day off?"

"Not if it means creeping around some

deserted building or hiding in a van."

"And if it means going away with me for a few days?"

"That could work," she replied.

"Who are you calling?" he asked when she reached for her cell.

"Work. I'll have to cancel a meeting if I'm not going to be there."

"Let's not," he husked. "Let's play hooky."

For a second, Raven had a moment of disquiet at his suggestion. No one would know where she was. If she got in trouble, no one would be coming to help. Giving herself a mental shake, she decided it was high time she trusted Mac. As Ash pointed out last night; he had done nothing to threaten or scare her. Mac had only ever offered comfort and protection. But to be honest, she conceded, she had a hard time trusting anyone following Derek's colossal betrayal.

"Trust me," Mac said offering her his hand. "I will never hurt you."

He was standing on a distant pinnacle asking her to ignore every self-preservation fiber in her being and join him, Raven mused. In the end, his look of hopeful appeal was her undoing; pulling on the heartstrings of a woman who had already fallen for him, but had yet to realize this on a conscious level. Throwing caution to the wind, she took his hand and joined him on the ledge. As his gaze transformed to love and affection, she heard herself saying, "I'm in."

EIGHTEEN

Sitting in his car outside Raven's brownstone, Brad watched as Mac stowed her small suitcase in the trunk of his car. Even in the dwindling light, he could tell Raven was excited about their weekend getaway. When they pulled away from the curb, Brad let three cars get ahead of him before he inched his way into traffic. He had been keeping tabs on Raven since the bug he planted on her suddenly went dead. The last GPS reading was an apartment off Michigan Avenue. He had dashed right over. Expecting to find another dead body; he had arrived just in time to see Mac bundle Raven securely in his car. He had followed them to an upscale house in Lincoln Park. He'd put in a call to his contact in records. He had been stunned to learn Mac was the owner of such an opulent home. A sure sign, Brad grimly thought, that Mac wasn't who he claimed to be. And now he was about to disappear with the only leverage that could be used against Luther.

Brad knew the Museum was reporting Raven was taking an unscheduled vacation. They offered the flimsy excuse that she needed time to come to grips with Stella's death. But he had questioned Museum staff extensively; listening to all the messy gossip that went on behind the scenes in the Museum. Charles seemed particularly torn about Stella's death. Alternating between weeping and belligerence, he reported that Stella and Raven were not close friends. According to Charles, they were barely on speaking terms; so the excuse to get out of the office because of Stella's demise, had to be Mac's idea.

Mac found the bug; so what, Brad reasoned. He couldn't pin anything on him. Anyone at the Station could have accidentally planted that harmless looking flower on Raven. Besides, Brad knew he could easily argue that he was on the case to keep Raven safe. With Stella and Gary out of the way, Raven was the obvious choice in enticing Luther out of hiding. He'd heard the rumor that Luther was supposedly working undercover when he disappeared. He could identify who was supplying pharmaceutical grade meth to Chicago's south side. Strange, Brad thought with a frown. He had never suspected Luther of being anything but an overzealous forensic student. Luther was a loose end that needed to be dealt with; and Raven was the sure-fire way of getting to him.

They had been driving for almost two hours when Mac began to merge into the far right lane. Grimacing when he suddenly increased his speed to take the exit ramp; Brad hit the gas to follow him off the highway. He realized he had been spotted when Mac's car veered out of the exit lane at the last minute. With the number of cars around him, Brad was forced to exit the highway or risk causing a five car pileup.

"Where did you learn to drive crazy man?" Raven asked; rattled by Mac's evasive maneuver.

"Quantico," he supplied succinctly.

Not sure how she felt about him zig zagging on the road like a drunk driver, she asked, "do you want me to drive?"

"We had a tail."

"Was it Brad?" she queried. Spooked beyond reason, she looked back to search the cars behind them. The search was futile because in the waning light all she could see were headlights.

"That would be my guess," Mac answered unperturbed. "He's been tailing us since we left Ashley's apartment."

"What!" she sputtered. "And you're just telling me this now?"

"Don't worry," he soothed. "I lost him. You don't get bragging rights at Quantico as the best dang wheel man for nothing," he boasted.

"I really don't want to be involved in a high speed car chase," she replied.

"Relax," he directed when she craned her neck around again.

"Oh, my gosh!" she yelped. "I think he's back there," she blurted slumping down in her seat.

"No, he's not," Mac soothed. "Trust me, I lost him."

"Are you sure?" she asked. "I saw a maroon car. It looked kinda sketchy."

"Brad's driving a black car."

"If this turns into a high speed chase, pull over and let me out. I'm pretty sure I can hoof it home from here."

Chuckling, he squeezed her hand

reassuringly. "You'll be fine."

"Where are you taking me?"

"Someplace safe," he promised.

"Not the same someplace safe you took Stella I hope?"

"No. I figured the best way to keep you safe is to not let you out of my sight."

"Maybe this isn't a good idea," she uttered as they crossed the Wisconsin border. "I'd feel a lot better if we stayed in the city Mac."

"The city is the first place Brad will seek you out. I'm sure he knows all of your haunts and habits by now."

"What about Ash? Will she be ok?"

"I have a protection detail on her."

"But what's in Wisconsin?" she wondered.

"You'll see," he cajoled.

"Um," she jerked. She felt herself growing tenser by the minute as their surroundings became more isolated.

"Why don't you close your eyes and relax,"

Mac suggested. "We'll be there before you know it."

"I'm too wired. I got an ex-seal gunning for me."

"I believe Brad was army Ranger," Mac casually replied.

"Can a seal take a ranger?" Raven asked.

"We would be equally matched. Hard to say who would come out on top. But don't worry," he directed at her frightened look. "We lost him. Once we get to the hotel, we'll blend in with everyone else like tourist. It will be impossible for Brad to track us."

"There'll be other people there?"

"Yes. The FBI does not have the budget to buy every room in the hotel."

"Um," Raven replied feeling herself slowly exhale.

Reclining her seat, she rested her head for mere seconds it seemed before she heard Mac announce cheerfully, "we're here!"

Startled, she looked around anxiously. She relaxed considerably when she saw the swank hotel.

For a moment, she'd thought Mac had brought her to the middle of nowhere; her bleached bones would be discovered in a ditch months later.

"You coming?" Mac smirked. A sure sign, Raven observed, that he was reading her again.

About to take issue with him reading her yet again, she asked instead, "where is here?" Mac had pulled up to a luxury hotel; a hotel that was out in the middle of nowhere.

"We're going glamping," he grinned.

"What's glamping?"

"Camping, but with all the amenities of a five-star hotel."

"Does that mean we're sleeping outside?" she asked feeling squeamish. With Brad on the loose, she wanted the security of walls and doors that locked between them.

"You're an archeologist. You go on remote digs all the time," he reminded.

"Yeah, but I don't have an ex-special force guy gunning for me on those digs. I don't know if staying in a tent is the smartest move. Maybe we should stay in the hotel."

"Don't worry," he assured her. "This is the best disguise ever." Retrieving their bags, he asked, "who would guess you were glamping?"

"No one," she conceded. Not even Ash would pick up on that one. "Boy," she chuckled softly. "When you say play hooky you really go all out; as in out in the middle of nowhere."

"We're only three hours from the city," he said. Taking her hand he led the way to check in.

"It feels like we're a day's ride on horseback away. I hope they have running water and showers here."

"We have all the modern amenities the receptionist replied. Let me give you a tour of the facilities."

She led them first to the dining room. It was set outdoors under a canopy of trees. The trees were strung with twinkling lights; while glass enclosed goblets were a featured center piece on each table. The twinkling lights and goblets provided rich ambient lighting. "Gosh," Raven whispered in awe.

"I thought you might like it here," Mac murmured at the sheer delight on her face.

"It's amazing," she said.

The receptionist then led them to the rustic fire pit. It was housed in a mammoth sized shelter. Adirondack chairs encircled the fire pit; while Chinese lanterns of varying sized hung from the shelter ceiling. They were finally led to the park like setting behind the hotel. The archway leading to their tent was illuminated by more twinkling lights and a glass enclosed goblet. The entire setting was breathtaking, Raven sighed. Entering their tent, she found a king sized bed; a hammock and another globular light fixture hanging from the ceiling.

"This is beautiful," she grinned. "How did you find this place?"

"This is the only type of camping my mom will do," he admitted. "Anything…"

"There's a phone!" Raven squealed when she spotted it on the night stand."

"And room service," he replied. "We don't have to eat in the dining room if you don't want."

"But it's so pretty," she sighed. "I want to try everything."

"Well in that case, we should check out the planned activities scheduled for tomorrow."

Studying the planned activity sheet, Raven

wrinkled her brow, "a boat ride on lake Michigan. Pass."

"What's wrong with that?"

"This far north in early November?" she queried. "It's going to be freezing on the water."

"What about rock climbing?"

"Pass. Here's one, cake decorating."

"Pass," Mac shuddered.

"But I thought you wanted to get to know me; the real me," she said with an exaggerated lisp.

"Seriously, is that how you think I sound?" he asked appalled.

"That's your cop voice," she smiled mischievously. "On a good day," she added gleefully.

"Why you little…" Lunging for her, Raven just escaped his grasp as she darted out of the tent.

Racing through the park, she tossed over her shoulder, "give it up G-man you'll never catch me." Seeing him gaining, she sprinted out of his reach. "I was all State throughout college," she harped seconds before she careened into him.

"You may have been all State," he purred smugly. "But I'm sneakier."

"How did you get in front of me?"

"Short cut," he grinned as he backed her to the nearest tree.

"What are you doing?"

"Claiming my reward," he husked on a throaty whisper. Swooping down, he captured her lips in a passionate kiss.

{}

Hearing the soft snap of a twig, Raven tensed immediately. Someone was out there, she reasoned. They were making a careful and stealthy approach to the tent. "Mac," she whispered uneasily when she heard the unmistakable crunch of gravel.

"What?" he growled sleepily.

"I heard a noise," she uttered urgently.

"It's the wind," he offered. He didn't want to alarm her, but he had been tracking the progression of someone sneaking ever closer to their tent for the past half hour. He had hoped Raven was asleep, but apparently, she wasn't.

"Someone is out there. I saw someone creeping slowly past our tent," she added tugging on his shoulder.

"We're glamping and bathrooms are indoors. Everyone will have to take the path to get to the bathrooms."

"It wasn't like that," she argued. "This was too close; like they were snooping around. It's Brad," she voiced her worse fear.

It definitely wasn't Brad, Mac conceded. The silhouette was all wrong. "I lost Brad miles from here. I'm sure it's nothing…" stilling suddenly when the lurking shadow loomed closer to their tent, Mac signaled her to be quiet. Getting stealthily out of bed, he grabbed his gun from the night table. He left the tent leaving Raven petrified staring at the tent opening.

"Hey…what the…" was voiced seconds before a muffled commotion outside. Raven sat shivering imagining her worse nightmare. Brad would probably bludgeon Mac before racing in to finish her off. Why hadn't they stayed in a hotel room like normal folk, she mused. She never should have let Mac talk her into sleeping outside in a tent with a killer on the loose; especially since she was on said killer's hit list.

Hearing a woman scream, Raven leaped out of bed and raced to the opening. She got there just in time to see Mac sheepishly lift a half-conscious man from the ground. "What have you done to my husband?" the woman screeched.

"I'm sorry ma'am. I thought he was an intruder."

"It's dark out here. He was looking for our tent and got lost," she bellowed. Looking around at the ample lighting and the number clearly illuminated on each tent, Mac looked at the woman shrewdly. Instinct told him she was lying. Dragging the man closer to the light, he recognized a known petty thief.

"FBI," Mac said in a very authoritative voice.

Startled, the woman turned and ran in the opposite direction. She left her semi-conscious husband to whatever fate the courts would mete out.

"There is never a dull moment with you," Raven said as she shook her head. "Even off duty, you make an arrest."

"What can I say," he grinned. "I am that good."

"Are you going to call it in?" she wondered.

"Can't, that would blow our cover. I'll turn him over to hotel security. They'll alert the local authorities."

When Mac half carried the semi-conscious intruder to hotel security, Raven returned to their tent. Oddly, she was somewhat mollified that the intruder was just a regular thief and not someone out to get her.

"That didn't take long," she voiced when Mac returned.

"Other glampers heard the commotion and phoned it in. Security was already on the way to our tent. They also caught the wife," he added as he secured the tent flap. "They're hauling them off to the poky even as we speak."

Crawling into bed Raven yawned, "good; because home girl here can't take anymore drama tonight."

"Not even a little footsie under the covers?" he husked.

"Shut up and get in bed," she chuckled. "We'll revisit footsie tomorrow when we're both alert enough to remember it."

"Promise," he asked hopefully.

"Promise," she murmured on a stifled yawn.

Mac doused the light and got into bed. Raven didn't demur when he reached for her. Cradled securely in his arms, she promptly fell asleep.

NINETEEN

"There you are," Charles bristled when Raven came out of the staff meeting on Monday. Apparently, he had been waiting in the hall; becoming more and more impatient as the meeting ran long. The tread in the carpet told her, he had been pacing frantically back and forth. "I've been looking for you all day."

"Why?" she asked. She was still in a paradise state of mind following her weekend with Mac. So she couldn't take Charles typical high strung behavior with any degree of urgency. The cake decorating class had been an eye opener. As the only man in the class, most of the women had gravitated towards him. But Mac had given her, his full undivided attention. She in turn had openly and publicly declared Mac as off limits. This was all

the encouragement he needed. He had unleashed
his full array of charm on her. They'd dined in that
ridiculously romantic dining room; sipped cider
while relaxing by the fire pit. Raven had even tried
her luck at rock climbing; and snuggled close to
Mac while gazing at the starry sky. All in all, it had
been a relaxing and romantic weekend, she recalled
with a dreamy smile.

"Will you take that silly grin off your face
and listen?" Charles demanded suddenly aggressive.

"What is your problem Charles?" Raven
asked equally aggressive. "You are not a member
of the curator's team, you are not my supervisor,
our work does not overlap, so what do you want?"

"Sorry," he backed down immediately. "It's
just that with Stella gone things have been…"
Heaving on a heavy sigh, he said, "that cop you're
on such friendly terms with was here earlier."

"Mac was here?" Raven asked surprised.
Why didn't he wait for me, she wondered; or in
typical Mac fashion, barge into the meeting.

"I don't know his name," Charles scowled.
"But you were on very good terms with him at the
Station," he spat.

"Okay," she replied coldly. "What is your

deal Charles? Mac could snap you like a twig in no time."

"He laughed at Stella. Now she's dead," he blustered.

"He was laughing at himself," she corrected. "And for the record, Mac did not harm Stella in any way."

"Whatever," he shrugged clearly not buying Mac's innocence. "Anyway, he wanted to meet you here," he said handing her a scrap of paper.

Looking at the address, Raven saw it was the apartment in North Lawndale. Why would Mac want to meet there, she frowned? Taking out her phone, she immediately called him. Unfortunately, the call went straight to voicemail.

"Is something wrong?" Charles asked of her baffled expression.

"Did he say why he wanted to meet at this address?"

"Not really," Charles shrugged. "But he was acting funny."

"How so?"

"Like he was here at the museum, but didn't

want to be seen. He said something had come up, that's why he couldn't wait for you."

"Um," she replied noncommittally. Had Mac finally located Luther?

"Is everything alright?" Charles wondered curiously.

"Yes, its fine," she murmured. "Er, thanks for letting me know Charles. I'll take it from here."

"Yes of course," he agreed. Turning towards accounting, he left her standing in the hall.

Making her way to her own office, Raven called Mac again. This time she left a detailed voice message telling him she'd gotten his message and was leaving the Museum to meet him in Lawndale. Grabbing her keys, she headed out the door.

{}

Parking in front of the building, Raven stared at the dilapidated site uneasily. Mac had better have a good reason for meeting in this dump, she shuddered. The place looked no more hospitable than the last time she was here. Exiting the car, she spotted Charles as he pulled in behind her.

"What are you doing here Charles?"

"I lost Stella by letting her go off alone. I won't let the same thing happen to you."

"I'll be fine," she assured him.

"I'm not taking any chances," he insisted. "No one knows you're here except that big guy from the station."

Blanching when she was Brad's car turn onto the street, she asked, "what did this cop look like, exactly?" she stressed.

"Big guy. Looked like an ex-marine or something, black…"

"Brad!" Raven screeched stiltedly. Suddenly afraid, she mouthed, "I thought you said Mac gave you the note."

"I said the cop you were friendly with at the Station," he defended. "I didn't catch his name."

Looking up and down the street, Raven noticed it was unusually deserted. Had it been like that when she pulled up?

"There he is," Charles announced unnecessarily when Brad parked and got out of his car. Picking up on Raven's agitation, he fretted, "what do we do?"

Sizing Charles up, Raven figured he would be useless in a street fight; and she could not take on Brad alone. Grabbing Charles' hand, Raven pulled him along as she dashed inside the building.

"Knock on doors Charles; make some noise!" she ordered. As they frantically knocked on doors, they continued their frantic progression up the stairs.

"No one is going to help us," he whined.

"Keep trying," Raven directed. Reaching apartment 3D, the door was yanked open before she could knock. "Luther!" she uttered completely surprised. But hearing Brad thundering up the steps behind them, she said, "Brad's here. He is just behind…"

"I'm so sorry Raven," Mac uttered with remorse. "I never wanted to hurt you."

"Mac what are you…" she began seconds before she saw his gun pointed directly at her. Before she could move or say another word, he pulled the trigger. Her look of shocked disbelief was the last thing Mac saw before she crumpled to the ground.

Darting up the stairs, with gun at the ready,

Brad stumbled upon the inert bodies of Charles and Raven. "Did you have to shoot her?" Brad asked cocking his gun at Mac.

"Didn't have a choice," Mac replied somberly. When he gently lifted Raven's body, Brad saw the grisly deranged smile plastered on Charles face. He also saw the gun held askew in his hand.

"Charles!" Brad thundered surprised. "He's the dealer?"

"Charles," Luther nodded. Further discussion was lost as emergency crew rushed up the stairs.

{}

The cold sterile room in the morgue was as bland as ever Luther decided. He was there to identify the body and he just wanted to get it over with. As the coroner droned on, he looked blankly ahead. He sat completely shell shocked at the outcome of events. When Brad entered the room, followed closely by Mac, he nearly flinched. "I can't believe you shot Raven," he uttered.

"Do you think I wanted to?" Mac slumped. "I'll never forget the look on her face."

"You shot her!" Luther stressed unappeased.

"Sometimes the only way to take out an opponent is to shoot through an ally," Brad interjected. "Mac actually saved Raven's life."

"Hmph," Luther snorted.

"Charles was livid Stella was taken and planned to take it out on Raven. He would have killed her if Mac hadn't stopped him. That's why he lured her to Lawndale. I think his plan was to make it look like a random act of violence," Brad said. "Fortunately, Raven had the forethought to call Mac to tell him where she was going. Mac in term called his contacts, who alerted me to the situation.

Gazing at Charles' diminutive body on the slab, Luther shook his head pitifully. "He was such an unassuming man."

"So was the Boston strangler," Brad noted.

"That is precisely how he managed to set up a drug ring from here to Mexico. Who would suspect a nerdy guy in receiving?" Mac said.

"But I didn't know anything about his drug ring," Luther protested. "Juanita and I stumbled across massive credit card fraud. We didn't even know what we had at first."

"Charles' fragile weak persona was an act. He was a ruthless killer who ruled his empire with a vicious hand. We were already monitoring the drug ring. Your intel put us on to him as a key player Luther. Thanks to you, we can dismantle his empire," Mac enlightened.

"You don't have to tell me he was ruthless," Luther offered. "He took out Juanita like it was nothing; like he was swatting a fly."

"Did Stella tell you anything?" Mac asked Brad.

"She gave me everything," he nodded. "I got date, times, routes the whole enchilada."

"What are you going to tell Raven?" Luther asked.

"Everything," Mac answered. "I'll be there when she wakes from surgery."

"We all will," Luther offered quietly.

{}

As the fog began to lift, Raven felt an excruciating pain. It radiated from her shoulder to the entire left side of her body. Trying to ease the pain, she shifted slightly. This intensified the pain ten-fold. She tried to scream, but something was jammed down her throat. Her eyes fluttered open. She found Mac sitting alone; staring at her worriedly. As memories returned, her blood pressure shot up. She remembered running for her life; and finding Luther in apartment 3D. Then Mac snuck up and shot her. He had undoubtedly left her for dead; the jerk, she fumed. If she survived this ordeal, she was going to remove his spleen. Nursing staff bustled in when her monitors began to bleep. They shooed Mac to the hall while they attempted to stabilize her vitals.

TWENTY

Raven surfaced eight hours later. People were standing around staring at each other worriedly. The excruciating pain was gone. In fact, she couldn't feel the left side of her body at all. Oh god I'm dead, she blenched! This must be my funeral.

"I can't believe you shot her!" Ashley snarled with venom. She was leaning aggressively towards Mac; held back by Luther's restraining hand.

The reaction to her clearing her throat was almost comical, Raven thought. They jumped slightly before turning to stare at her with concern. The intubation tube had been removed and her throat was killing her. It felt like the tube had been ripped out, leaving her throat lacerated and raw.

Mac reached her first. Leaning over her carefully, he asked somberly, "how are you feeling?"

"Water," she rasped weakly.

Mac moved with alacrity and placed a straw gently to her lips. After a few painful sips, she nodded that she was done. "What happened?" she croaked hoarsely.

As everyone clamored around her, Ashley jerked in Mac's direction, "he shot…"

"I got this," Mac said before she could finish.

Ash was about to take issue with Mac commandeering the conversation, but the gentle tug from Luther quieted her down. "Right," Luther interjected into the awkward silence. "Ash and I will head for the cafeteria for coffee. Cream no sugar Mac?" Luther asked.

"Yeah, that's fine," he murmured distractedly. When Luther and Ash left the room, Mac took a seat at her bedside.

"I can't feel my arm," Raven uttered terrified.

"It's alright," Mac soothed. "The bullet…it

was a clean shot," he admitted uneasily. "You'll be in pain for a while, but you'll make a full recovery."

"Why can't I feel my arm?"

"It's the pain meds. You were coming out of anesthesia rapidly. Your blood pressure shot through the roof as your pain increased. Since your vitals were stable, they increased the pain meds for your arm."

"Um," she replied trying to wiggle her fingers.

"You'll need some physical therapy, but you are going to be okay."

"No thanks to you," she muttered.

"I'm sorry Raven. But I couldn't let him take you out like that. I had one shot. I had to take it," he uttered with remorse.

"Was it Brad?" she wondered curiously.

"Charles," he said as her eyes widened in shock.

"Ch…Charles!" she sputtered in disbelief. "He's a total weenie."

"That was his façade," Mac corrected. "In reality he was a psychopath who enjoyed killing…"

"But…"

"Let me explain," Mac said placing a gentle finger on her lips. "Chicago PD has known about Stella's credit card fraud for the past 6 months. They were tracking her activities to take down her entire crew. It was Luther and Juanita who accidentally stumbled across the drug smuggling scheme." At her questioning look, he said, "they were using the art arriving at the museum; anything exotic was a target."

"Is that why Stella volunteered to check in all shipments and follow up with customs paperwork?" Raven wondered.

"Yes," Mac confirmed. "And it wasn't just West African Art. We found contraband throughout the museum. Stella with Charles' help, monitored receiving religiously. They wanted to get the contraband out before anyone noticed something amiss." He paused briefly letting her digest the information. When she nodded for him to continue he said, "Brad was in charge of the investigation. Problem is, Chicago PD has no jurisdiction outside of Chicago. That's why he brought in the FBI."

"You're really FBI then?" Raven asked.

"Yes," Mac nodded. "I went in undercover; but Stella was suspicious and very careful. We needed to shake things up; Luther…"

"I knew is," she hissed. "I knew you put my brother in danger."

"He was never in any real danger," Mac assured her. "The police and FBI were in full control of the situation."

"So why did he call me; and send me to that Lawndale building?"

"Er, we were in full control of the situation most of the time," Mac shrugged. "Luther panicked when he saw Juanita murdered. It was a rookie mistake."

"Um," Raven hmphed.

"Anyway, Luther was to meet Stella for a fraudulent credit card. Juanita was tagging along just to add credibility to his story."

"So what happened?"

"The plan went south. Stella didn't show; Charles did. This was the first time anyone had connected Charles to anything. We weren't sure if he was a key player or Stella's fall guy."

"What do you mean?"

"At first he was twittery and weak as if he

was there under duress. He kept fidgeting with his duffel bag as if he wasn't sure Luther could be trusted. When he recognized Juanita as a reporter; and worse, she was wired. He morphed into a deranged psychopath in an instant."

"How?"

"Juanita's death was overkill. She was shot nine times and stabbed twenty-seven. Even when she was dead on the floor, he kept stabbing her like a deranged nut bar."

"Ugh," Raven shuddered.

"His behavior freaked Luther out. But his psychotic behavior was the distraction Luther used to get out. He grabbed the duffel bag and legged it."

"And Stella?"

"Feared for her life from that moment on. She knew one slip up and she would be the one lying cut up on the floor."

"Why was she so scared of you?"

"Charles told her I was the one who gutted Juanita. She believed him at first. But as time went on, she began to question his sanity."

"Why?"

"He was prone to fits of maniacal giggling for no reason. And he kept bringing up the grisly details of Juanita's death; details that only the actual killer would have. Stella thought he was trying to scare her, but I think he thought she was like minded."

"Which she wasn't," Raven shuddered.

"No, she wasn't; but that was something Charles was unable to comprehend. Talking about a grisly murder was his way of wooing her. He also kept her on a short leash; hoping she would come to love the same psychotic things that he did."

"So, Stella was kinda in a mentally abusive relationship," Raven noted.

"Of her own making," Mac replied. "She also set Luther and Juanita up. She had to know Charles was a very dangerous man."

"Why was Juanita wired?"

"Amateur mistake. She was trying to break the fraud story before we had sufficient evidence to dismantle the entire empire. We didn't want to stop Stella in Chicago; only to have her resurface with a new name and operation in Miami. And we didn't know about Charles until that night."

"And Stella, what happened to her?"

"She really is in witness protection," Mac assured her.

"Then she's not dead?"

"Far from it." At her bemused look, he said, "that report on the news was a plant. Stella knew Charles was watching her every move and she wanted out. She had firsthand knowledge of his entire operation and she was scared."

"When you told us she got away…"

"I was trying to draw Charles out; and letting Brad know Stella was at the safe house. That was his cue to question her and offer the witness protection deal."

"Which she took."

"Yes."

"Is that why Charles was always coming to the stockroom?" Raven wondered.

"To be honest, I think he genuinely had a thing for Stella. He thought she was like him; that she put on a professional façade to get through the day. She was his anchor in the sane world. When she went missing he really fell apart."

"What about Gary, who killed him?"

"We can't prove it yet, but we think Charles planted the bomb on Baymiller. Gary was a loose end he was tying up. But Gary's death completely spooked Stella; it sent her right into our waiting arms."

"You never sent that message for me to meet you in Lawndale?" she asked.

"No. Charles wanted you alone. My guess is he was itching for another kill and he didn't much care who it was. I think he planned to mutilate you as he did with Juanita."

"But why? We weren't enemies."

"Like I said, Stella kept him sane. When she was no longer there, he gave in to his dark and sadistic nature. His basement was full of animal mutilations. Rabbits, cats, dogs, squirrels… it was sick."

"I'm glad you got there in time then."

"Letting me know where you were going was a very smart move. I wasn't sure if I'd get there in time; which is why I called Brad for back up."

"Seeing Brad really spooked me," she

voiced.

"I know. I'm sorry," Mac replied gravely.

Thinking things through Raven asked, "if you and Brad were on the same side; why did he plant a bug in my purse?"

"Deep undercover means deep cover and you don't break cover. Brad thought I had gone rogue. He wasn't sure if I was operating as an FBI agent, or had fallen under Charles' thumb. He was trying to keep you safe."

"Was he really following us when we went glamping?"

"He was but I lost him."

"Stella told me about your cousin. The one that tried to fly…"

Halting her with a raised hand, he said, "a fabrication, part of my cover story."

"And us, was that part of your cover story?" she voiced grimly.

"No," he replied immediately. "I've wanted you since I saw your picture in Luther's wallet."

"Really?" she asked with a wide grin.

"Yes really," he said. Gazing at her with tender affection, he added, "but Luther was not down with us getting together."

"Why?" Raven asked surprised.

"He thought my profession was too dangerous for you; that you would be better off with a librarian or accountant; someone unassuming."

"Like Charles?"

"I'm betting after his encounter with Charles, he's rethinking the FBI angle."

Leaning forward as Mac carefully adjusted her pillow, she asked, "where was Luther this whole time?"

"Mostly he stayed in my apartment in Wickers...."

"What!" Raven rasped. "I was a nervous wreck and you couldn't tell me this was all an act?"

"I was undercover..." Ducking, he just missed the water jug as it was hurled at his head.

"You jerk," she blared. "You could have told me something."

"My first priority was keeping you safe. The less you knew, the less chance you had of

286

becoming a target."

"When you came to my apartment that morning, was Luther really missing?"

"Yes," Mac answered. "And just so you know, I was sick with worry. Our simple credit card fraud case had suddenly gone sideways."

"Why weren't you with Luther when he went to get the card?"

"It wasn't a dangerous mission. About fifty students from the University have received fraudulent credit cards from Stella. This was supposed to be routine. When Luther saw what was in the duffel bag, he nearly lost his water. His first mission out and he stumbled across a drug ring.'

"When did you have Luther secured?" Raven wondered.

"Uh, when I stopped at your place to make you coconut chicken," he replied sheepishly. "Analysis of the drugs in the duffel bag showed it was the same junk being sold in Chicago south side."

"You knew from that day onward that Charles was the man at the top?"

"Yes," Mac shrugged ruefully. "With

Luther, safe and me watching over you, we had our best chance of dismantling the entire operation. Remember there was a leak in the department; which is why Brad brought in the FBI. We have arrested the captain and seven police officers so far. We were also working to turn Stella. Once she turned State's evidence, we were ready to take Charles down."

"Why didn't you? What happened?"

"His need for another kill is what happened?" Mac replied. "It was a sloppy move luring you to that building. He thought if he arrived separately no one would connect your death to him."

"What a sick-o," Raven shuddered.

"He failed to realize that I was not about to leave you unprotected. Sadie was keeping an eye on you."

"The cat lady!" Raven screeched.

"That's her cover. Her real name is Katrina Boudin. She's actually a cop and only thirty-three years old. Plus, she's well versed in martial arts and a very good shot."

"The cat lady!" she screeched again in wonderment.

"A homeless person is an ideal cover. They can gain access to just about any venue and people try not to notice them."

"Is that why I kept running into her?" she asked ruefully.

"Yeah," Mac grinned. "I asked her to keep an eye on you. She thought her cover was blown when you saw her at the station coming out of the ladies' room."

"I didn't think anything of it," Raven shrugged. "I thought she was sneaking in to use the bathroom and that's all."

"I take it she knows everything now," Luther grinned as he entered the room.

"Pretty much," Mac replied taking the coffee Luther held out to him.

EPILOGUE

"That's the last of 'em," Raven heaved as she closed the lid on the final suitcase with a definite snap.

"I'll take that," Ash warned as she relieved Raven of the small suitcase. "I don't want Mac going kamikaze on me."

Raven had been out of the hospital for several weeks. She had moved in with Ashley during her recuperation; and had watched Mac morph from big tough navy Seal to over protective nurse maid. Although she had found his behavior endearing at first, he was now driving her batty. She was feeling better and had decided to move back to her own apartment, much to Mac's horror.

"Maybe once I'm back at my place he'll

calm down," Raven soothed.

"I seriously doubt that," Ashley snorted. "It's always the big ones hiding their inner nurse maid," she said as she placed the suitcase with Raven's belongings by the door. "But I am going to miss having you here," she teased.

"Please," Raven offered. "With the ruckus you and Luther make throughout the night, its indecent having me in the next room." Luther's disappearance had spooked Ash to the point that she'd declared her love for him the second he was out of hiding. Luther had confessed that the whole time he was away, all he could think about was Ashley. They were now a happy couple in the grips of a passionate affair. Raven thought if she had to witness more of their passion, she'd puke for sure.

"What?" Ash asked innocently. "It's a beautiful and natural thing."

"Just so you know," Raven mouthed sarcastically. "It is possible to know way too much about your love life."

"I guess you don't want to know our birth control method?" she grinned.

"Ugh, god no!" Raven shuddered dramatically. "And can we please change the subject? I'm getting hives from this one."

"What evs," Ash dismissed. "What time is Mac picking you up?"

"He said around 3:30. Why?"

"I need to check my storage unit for streamers and I need to go through that box on the sofa to see what favors I'm short on. Can you go through the box while I check the storage unit downstairs?"

"Will do," Raven replied as Ash left the room.

Despite her vehement protesting, Ash was throwing her a going home party. Raven had insisted the party was overkill. But aided and abetted by Luther and a guilt ridden Mac; the party was moving full steam ahead.

Sitting comfortably on the sofa, she sifted through party favors. There were about thirty or more that were in good condition. Typical Ash fashion, Raven thought with a rueful shake of her head. She was going completely overboard for something that should have been a quiet dinner with friends. Caught up with sorting, Raven didn't notice Mac entering the room.

"Aw come on!" he voiced in mock chagrin.

"Just what is it going to take for you to take it easy?"

"It's been eight weeks," Raven excused. "But you're right. You shot me. Just look at my arm," she replied. Jiggling it weakly she said, "I still don't have the proper use and strength in this arm." Coughing dramatically, she leaned against the sofa weakly. "Luther is that you?" she uttered as if she was taking her last breath. "Come into the light so I can see you properly," she wheezed.

Rolling his eyes heavenward Mac asked, "okay, what'd ya want?"

Hiding her smug grin, Raven sprung up with alacrity. "For starters, I want you to stop babying me; and if you're going to insist on this party, let me help. Ashley is doing way too much."

"The doctor said you are not to overdo things. Your shoulder needs to heal…"

"But he doesn't want her arm to wither," Ash inserted as she carried a box of streamers into the room.

"I give up," Mac heaved looking between the two of them. Knowing he was not going to win this battle he changed tactics and asked, "what can I do to help?"

"Raven tells me you are an excellent cook. That means you're on hors d'oeuvre detail."

"Help me in the kitchen Raven?" he asked with a quirk of his brow in her direction.

"Okay," she responded rising from the sofa. "Stop it," she directed at Ashley in response to the knowing smirk on her face.

"Maybe it's good you're going home now," she simpered. "I don't think Luther could handle hearing strange noises emanating from your bedroom," she chuckled.

"Ew gross," Raven tossed as she followed Mac into the kitchen.

Alone in the kitchen, Mac gathered her gently in his arms and held her tight. "How are you feeling?" he asked as he gently kneaded her shoulder blades.

"I'm fine Mac."

"Are you sure you're up to going back to your place alone?" he questioned urgently.

"For the hundredth time, yes I am Mac."

"But what if…"

"No if ands or buts about it," she insisted.

"I'm fine. You know yourself I can take care of myself," she reminded. "We were in a street fight together, remember?" Feeling him relax at her calm insistence that she was ready to be on her own, she snuggled closer.

"Well in that case you owe me," he rumbled softly.

Pulling back to stare at him in astonishment she asked, "how do you figure?"

"Our date," he reminded. "You said you wanted this mess with Luther cleared up before we started dating seriously."

"Hmmmm," Raven teased. "You know I don't recall agreeing to any such thing."

"Well you did."

"Says you," she shrugged. "You got any witnesses or anything that would hold up in court?"

"No," he smiled. "But I do have this?" Switching on his phone recorder, Raven's voice rang out clearly saying she didn't want to get involved until the mess with Luther was cleared up.

"Oh, my g g gosh!" she sputtered. "You recorded me? You are such a cop."

"FBI," he corrected distractedly. "I'm just covering all my bases," he teased.

"Since you have evidence, I suppose we could go out just this one time…you know to see if we are compatible," she offered.

"That sounds like a plan," he nodded. "We're, just making sure there is some chemistry there," he husked as he crowded her against the counter.

"We should probably just kiss right here and now," she murmured. "I mean no point in wasting gas mileage if there's no chemistry."

"You took the words right out of my mouth," he husked; seconds before he crushed her lips in a passionate kiss.

Ashley walked into the kitchen to give Mac a list of preferred hors d'oeuvre for the party. Finding him in the throes of a searing kiss with Raven, she quietly placed the list on the counter and returned to the living room.

-The End-

Also by Amethyst Hue

-The Balance of Trust-

-In The Balance-

-In The Balance-

...Recalling their time together, Derek smiled...running in the rain to catch the El; pooling their loose change to share a slice of pizza; strolling through the botanical gardens and heated arguments about the efficacy of the Lincoln Park Zoo, or as Raven called it – animal jail he mused with a soft chuckle.

Gwen snuggling close to her brown Adonis was happily planning their future. She saw them in the suburbs with three maybe four children. Feeling his soft chuckle, she husked, "what are you thinking?"

"I'm thinking about Raven," he dreamily replied. Derek realized his colossal mistake when the woman at his side went rigid. "Now Gwen," he tried to soothe.

"What!" she bellowed. Tossing aside the comforter she got out of bed to glare at him with open hostility. "Raven!" she spat as if the name was a nasty curse on her lips. "You're thinking about Raven when you're in bed with me?"

Unperturbed by her angst Derek shrugged, "now that we're back in Chicago everything reminds me of her. I was just wondering what she's up to right now."

Irritated beyond reason Gwen shouted, "why would you care what she's up to? We've been together for three and a half years. I thought you were over her! I thought you chose me!" she flung at him angrily.

"I never chose you," he corrected. "We just sort of fell together. I never stopped caring for Raven," he commented watching her flinch. Derek seemed incapable of realizing that his casual words were a direct blow to the heart. "If you recall, I'm here to launch my political career. Having someone like Raven by my side may be just the ticket to success."

"She's engaged," Gwen hissed.

"She was equally engaged when you made your play for me," he reminded.

"Do you know how much I've sacrificed for you?" she demanded. "If you think you can toss me aside like some random gutter snipe after all this time, you can very well think again," she threatened.

"What makes us such an effective team Gwen is that we understand each other. I will get to the top at all cost," he voiced sternly. "Get in my way and I will bury you," he warned.

"Your political career won't get half an inch without me," she derided. "I can derail your career with two words to the media. Like that!" she shouted with an angry snap of her fingers.

"How do you figure?" he wondered looking at his nails. Tomorrow he'd have his assistant schedule him a manicure. His nails were starting to look ragged.

Livid she'd lost his attention to something as inane as his fingernails Gwen angrily spewed, "I'm pregnant you selfish pig!"

ABOUT THE AUTHOR

Amethyst Hue currently resides in the
Midwest. Although no longer a resident of
Chicago she will always have a great and
abiding love for all things Chicago. She
continues to hone her writing skills in the
rural Midwest.

Made in the USA
Las Vegas, NV
09 November 2021

34055619R00171